Paddington Children's Hospital

Caring for children—and captivating hearts!

The doctors and nurses of
Paddington Children's Hospital are renowned
for their expert care of their young patients,
no matter the cost. And now, as they face
both a heart-wrenching emergency and a
dramatic fight to save their hospital,
the stakes are higher than ever!

Devoted to their jobs, these talented professionals
are about to discover that saving lives can often
mean risking your heart…

Available now in the thrilling
Paddington Children's Hospital miniseries:

Their One Night Baby by Carol Marinelli

Forbidden to the Playboy Surgeon by Fiona Lowe

Mommy, Nurse…Duchess? by Kate Hardy

Falling for the Foster Mom by Karin Baine

Healing the Sheikh's Heart by Annie O'Neil

A Life-Saving Reunion by Alison Roberts

Dear Reader,

This is the first time I have written in a proper continuity straight from the heart of Harlequin's Medical Romance editorial team at True Love Towers, and let me tell you—I'd do it again in a heartbeat!

I absolutely adored writing this book and working with the other wonderful authors. What a fabulous experience, much like working in a hospital with a smart, engaging, funny, busy-falling-in-love team of doctors. I know it's an oft-trotted-out line that a writer's profession is a lonely one, but this job certainly wasn't. It was definitely a group experience and so much the better for it (in my humble opinion!). I became so engaged in the world at Paddington Children's Hospital, I even ran a half marathon for Great Ormond Street Hospital, London's premier (real-life) hospital for children. And I'm no athlete. It took a while, but it was worth it. I hope you find yourself enjoying "working" your way through this series as much as I enjoyed writing *Healing the Sheikh's Heart*.

Remember not to be shy. I love hearing from readers. You can find me on Facebook and Twitter (@annieoneilbooks) and on my website: annieoneilbooks.com.

Happy reading!

Annie O'

HEALING THE SHEIKH'S HEART

ANNIE O'NEIL

ISBN-13: 978-0-373-21532-4

Healing the Sheikh's Heart

First North American Publication 2017

Copyright © 2017 by Harlequin Books S.A.

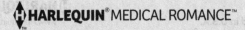

HARLEQUIN® MEDICAL ROMANCE™

Recycling programs
for this product may
not exist in your area.

Special thanks and acknowledgment are given to Annie O'Neil for her contribution to the Paddington Children's Hospital series.

ISBN-13: 978-0-373-21532-4

Healing the Sheikh's Heart

First North American Publication 2017

Copyright © 2017 by Harlequin Books S.A.

Printed in U.S.A.

Books by Annie O'Neil

Harlequin Medical Romance

Hot Latin Docs

✓ Santiago's Convenient Fiancée

Christmas Eve Magic

✓ The Nightshift Before Christmas

The Monticello Baby Miracles

✓ One Night, Twin Consequences

✓ One Night...with Her Boss
One Night, Most Eligible Doctor
✓ Her Hot Highland Doc

Visit the Author Profile page
at Harlequin.com for more titles.

This one is for all the gals who worked on the series. I was a first-timer and you made it a wonderful experience. A special shout-out to the fabulous Fiona Lowe, who always helps me keep my head screwed on, and Karin Baine, my partner in googly-eyes.

**Praise for
Annie O'Neil**

"This is a beautifully written story that will pull you in from page one and keep you up late turning the pages."

—*Goodreads* on *Doctor…to Duchess?*

**Annie O'Neil won the 2016 RoNA Rose Award
for her book *Doctor…to Duchess?***

CHAPTER ONE

"Next!"

Sure, it was clichéd, but so was the interview Idris had been forced to bring to an abrupt halt. How superficial did these people think he was?

His name on a hospital wing for having his daughter's surgery at the Chelsea Children's Clinic? *Ridiculous.* The money wasted on ribbon-cutting ceremonies and plaques should be spent on the children. In hospital. Wasn't that the point of a large donation? Not lavish displays of wealth and largesse. He had one concern and one concern only—bringing the gift of sound into his little girl's silent world. He turned at the gentle *ahem* prompt from Kaisha, all too aware this was exactly the sort of thing Amira couldn't experience.

"Are you ready for the next one?"

"Are there many more? I don't know how much more of this misplaced adulation I can take."

His assistant appeared by his side, scanning the printouts on her leather-clad clipboard. The one with the royal crest that always ramped up the anxious-to-please smiles of his interviewees.

Surgeons at the top of their games! He sucked in an embarrassed breath on their behalf, using the three-two-one exhale to try to calm himself.

"No, Your Excellency. We've only got three more."

"Kaisha, please." He only just stopped himself from snapping. "It's *Idris* when we're alone. There's only so much sycophancy a man can take in a day. You, of all people, know how important it is we find the right doctor for Amira."

"Yes, Your… Idris." Kaisha winced, did a variation of a curtsy, then threw her arms up in the air with the futility of getting it right and left the room. They both knew there was no need for a curtsy. They both knew Idris's glowering mood was virtually impossible to lift. He'd worn his "thunder face," as Amira liked to call it, near enough every day for the past seven years.

Despite his headache, an overdose of London's medical glitterati and a growing need to get out and stride off his frustration in one of London's sprawling royal parks, Idris smiled. Kaisha was loyal, intelligent and the last person he should be venting his frustration on. He'd hired her because she specialized in Da'har's rich history. Not for her skills as a PA. Perhaps he should hire her a PA to take up the slack.

He cupped his chin, stretching his neck first one way, then the next, willing the tension of the day to leave him…if not the penthouse suite altogether.

He crossed the impressive expanse of the suite's main sitting room. The "trophy suite" no less. Even he had winced at the pompous moniker but the location and views were incomparable. Nothing was off the shelf at Wyckham Place. Handcrafted tables, bespoke art pieces hung to match the modern, but undeniably select, furnishings and decor. He lived a life of privilege and preferred this type of understated elegance to flashy shows of gold-plated wealth. Apart from which, Amira liked the view of the London Eye and the Houses of Parliament the penthouse suite afforded. Anything to bring a smile to his little girl's face. She was so serious all the time. Little wonder, he supposed, without a mother's tender care and a father more prone to gravitas than gaiety.

His eyes hit a mirror as they left the view— the image confirming his thoughts. Hard angles, glinting eyes and the glower of a man with the weight of the world on his shoulders. There was a time when all he would've seen in return was a broad smile. When life was little short of perfect.

His gaze snagged on his grimace. Losing his wife had all but ripped his easily won grin straight from his face.

He looked away. Self-reflection had been another casualty. All that remained was his daughter's happiness and the well-being of Da'har. If a nation's character could run in a man's genes he knew he embodied all that the small Gulf nation stood for. Pride. Strength. Resilience.

His dark eyes hit the solid door of the suite, beyond which were two of his most trusted employees. Beyond them, at the lift, two more. And in the foyer of the hotel more waited, innocuously, in plain clothes. They were meant to provide a sense of security. Today it felt stifling.

A sudden urge overtook him to tug on a hat and walk out into the streets of London, bodyguards left behind none the wiser, and become... no one in particular. But finding the right surgeon for his daughter was paramount. He'd tolerate near enough anything for her. Even torture by fawning hospital officials. He was mortal, after all. A true god would have foreseen the complications his wife had endured during the birth of their beautiful daughter. A truer one would have saved her.

"How long has Amira been at the zoo?" Idris called over his shoulder.

Kaisha appeared by his side again. "Only an hour or so, Your—Idris. As you requested, they cleared the zoo of other patrons so Amira could have a private tour."

He wondered, fleetingly, how Kaisha did that.

Just…appeared. Maybe she'd been in the room the entire time and he simply hadn't noticed. One of his recently "acquired" traits.

Not so recent, he reminded himself. The seven longest years of his life. The only light in that time? His beautiful daughter.

"Excellent. Amira always takes ages with the giraffes and penguins. And remember, I don't want her anywhere near the hotel until we find the right person. If I have to pay to keep the zoo open longer, that's not a problem."

Even Idris didn't miss the pained expression Kaisha tried to hide from him as she lifted her clipboard to hide her features.

"What is it, Kaisha?"

"It's just…"

"Out with it!" Patience might be a virtue but it was most likely because it was in short supply. Particularly in his hotel suite.

"You've seen most of the specialists already and haven't bothered to hear any of them out."

"They all seemed more interested in attaching the Al Khalil name to their hospitals—or the Al Khalil money, rather—than in my daughter. She's the entire point of this exercise. Cutting-edge medicine. The best money can buy. Not getting my name spread across London! If Amira hadn't wanted to see that musical I would've flown everyone to Da'har and not wasted my time."

Kaisha, to her credit, nodded somberly. She had heard it all before. In between each of the interviews today, in fact. And the day before. Any patience in the room was Kaisha's alone. Idris was more than aware he had a tether and was swiftly approaching the very end of it.

"Right! It's the next person on the list or we're off to Boston Pediatrics or New York ENT. Enough of this nonsense. All right?"

"Yes, Your Ex— Idris." Kaisha gave a quick smile, proud to have remembered the less formal address in the nick of time. "Shall I fetch the next candidate?"

"We might as well get it over with," Idris grumbled, settling back into the only chair that comfortably accommodated his long limbs. "Who is it, please?"

"Uh—yes, sorry—it's Robyn Kelly. Dr. Robyn Kelly. *Salaam Alaikum.*"

Idris looked up sharply. The voice answering him was most definitely not Kaisha's.

Alssamawat aljamila!

The pair of eyes unabashedly meeting his own were the most extraordinary color.

Amber.

Lit from within just as a valued piece of the fossilized resin would be if it were held up to the sun. Mesmerizing.

The sharp realization that he was staring, responding to this woman in a way he had only done once before, made him bite out angrily, though she bore no blame for his transgression.

"How did you get in here?"

"Walked," she answered plainly, her wayward blond curls falling forward as she looked down. "With these." She pointed at her feet, clad in the sort of trainers he would've expected to see on a teenager. His eyes shot back to hers when he heard her giggling as if he had just asked the silliest question in the world.

"Oh!" She popped a finger up as a sign he should take note. "Your...I think they're your bodyguards...kindly let me in to 'powder my nose' a few minutes early. Hope that was all right. And it's Robyn with a *y* not an *i*—i.e., not like the little birdie up in the trees but pretty close! Blame my parents," she finished with a playful shrug.

He narrowed his eyes, assessing the new arrival as coolly as he could considering she looked about as dangerous as a baby lamb. Even so, no one got past his bodyguards. Ever. And yet this amber-eyed sylph had done just that. What if she'd found Amira and stolen her away? His heart seized at the thought.

Pragmatics forced him to blink away the foolish notion with a stern reminder that this... "Robyn"...was very human and that his daughter was safe and well.

His gaze returned to Robyn. A couple of inches above average height. About his age—midthirties. Slender. At least what he could see of her, as most of her body was hidden beneath an oversize trench coat that would've been stylish if she'd bought the correct size or used the belt as intended rather than as a long rope to swing round and round like an anxious cowgirl as she awaited his response. A wild spray of golden curls. Untamed. A makeup-free face. Evidence the "nose-powdering" was a euphemism. Her cheeks were pink...with the cold, perhaps? By Da'harian standards, the day was wintry. A three-year stint at an English university had taught him the on-again, off-again late-summer rainstorms were normal. In keeping with the storm-tossed treetops quaking along the riverbanks below, Robyn Kelly was looking similarly windswept and ever so slightly unkempt.

Perhaps more faerie or wayward pixie than sylph, then.

The mythical creatures, he suspected, didn't giggle. Nor did they tug their fingers through their hair when it was too late to make a good first impression.

Even so—he shifted in his seat—it was easy enough to picture Robyn in gossamer with a set of diaphanous wings taking flight over the palace gardens of Da'har.

Mercifully, he caught a glimpse of Kaisha appearing, and gave his throat a quick clear as if it would shunt away the images Robyn's presence elicited.

Kaisha shot an apologetic look at Idris. She didn't seem to know how Robyn had entered the suite any more than he did. "Dr. Kelly, could we offer you some coffee or—"

"Bless you, love! I'd kill for a good old-fashioned cup of builder's." Robyn's face lit up with a bright smile at Kaisha's instantly furrowed brow. "Apologies!" She laughed. "I forget English is your...what is it—third or fourth language?"

"Fourth." Kaisha smiled shyly.

"Fourth! I should be so lucky." Robyn's amber eyes flicked to Idris as if to say, *Can you believe this girl?*

"And such different languages, as well. If I remember from our emails, you have the Da'har dialect, Arabic, French and English?"

Kaisha nodded.

"Impressive. The only other language I speak is 'menu.' Builder's *tea*," Robyn explained, hardly pausing for breath. "It means brewed strong and with a healthy dollop of milk."

"Not cream?"

"No, love." Robyn shook her head with a gentle smile. "I'm not so posh as all that. And if you have a couple of biccies tucked away in there somewhere so much the better." She turned on the heel of what the cool kids would call her "trendy kicks" to face Idris. "I'm sorry. This is all a bit whirlwindy of me, isn't it? Shall I begin again? A bit more officially?" She stuck out her hand without waiting for an answer. "Dr. Kelly from Paddington Children's Hospital and you are…?"

"Sheikh Idris Al Khalil," he answered, rising to his full height and accepting her proffered hand, bemused to have to introduce himself at all.

"Great!" Robyn gave his hand a quick, sharp shake and just as quickly extracted her hand with a little wriggle as if he'd squeezed it too hard and not the other way around. "Amira's father." Her eyes darted around the room as she spoke. "Excellent. All right if I just throw my mac here on the sofa or would you rather I grab a hanger from somewhere so you could hang it up on…?" Her eyes continued to scan the room for an appropriate place to hang her soaked raincoat while he found himself completely and utterly at a loss for words.

No one had asked him to lift so much as a finger for them since…ever. Not that he minded lending a hand to a person in need, but…her lack of interest in his position in the Middle East, let alone the world, was refreshing. If not slightly disarming.

He arched an eyebrow as she twisted around,

untangling herself from the tan overcoat and about three meters' worth of hand-knitted scarf, muttering all the while about "British summers."

She pulled off the coat, managing to get an arm stuck in one of the sleeves, went through a microscopic and lightning-speed thought process before, rather unceremoniously, yanking her arm out and turning the sleeve inside out in the process. She gave an exasperated sigh, bundled the whole coat up with the scarf and tossed it into the corner of the überchic sofa before flopping onto the other corner in a show of faux despair.

He felt exhausted just watching her. And not a little intrigued.

Idris flicked his eyes away from Robyn's, finding the golden glow of them a bit too captivating. More so than her ensemble: a corduroy skirt that had seen the washing machine more than a few times, a flowered top with a button dangling precariously from a string. The trainers… More student than elite surgeon.

She was a marked contrast to the four preceding candidates who had all looked immaculate. Expensive suits. Silk ties. Freshly polished shoes. All coming across as if their mothers had dressed them for their first day at school. He huffed out a single, mirthless laugh. Little good it had done them.

"What? Is there something wrong?" Robyn

asked, her gaze following his to her cream-colored top dappled with pink tulips, a flush of color hitting her cheekbones when her eyes lit on a stain.

"Ah! Apologies!" she chirped, then laughed, pulling her discarded, well-worn leather satchel up from the ground where she'd dropped it when she came in and began digging around for a moment before triumphantly revealing a half-used supersize packet of wipes. "We just had congratulations cupcakes at the hospital for one of the surgeons who's newly engaged and I shared one with a patient while we were reading and—" she threw up her hands in a *What can you do?* gesture "—frosting!"

She took a dab at the streak of pink icing with a finger and he watched, mesmerized, as the tip of her tongue popped out, swirled around her finger, then made another little swipe along her full lower lip. "Buttercream. I just love that stuff! Doesn't stop the children from getting it absolutely everywhere, though, does it?"

She began scrubbing at her top with the wipe, chattering away as she did. "Bless them. Being in hospital is bad enough, but having to worry about manners?" She shrugged an indecipherable response into the room, clearly not expecting him to join in on the one-sided conversation. "Then again, if the hospital weren't on the brink of closing I probably wouldn't be here making a class-A idiot out of myself. I'd be in surgery where I belong."

Her eyes flicked up and met his.

"Uh-oh." Her upper teeth took hold of her full lower lip as her face creased into an apologetic expression. "Out-loud voice?" Again, she didn't wait for an answer, shook her head and returned to her task. "That's what they get for sending the head of surgery and not PR!"

Idris watched near openmouthed, trying to divine if *she* was mad or if *he* was for letting her ramble on, all the while dabbing her blouse a bit too close to the gentle swell of her...

He forced his gaze away, feeling his shoulders cinch and release as Robyn's monologue continued unabated. She hadn't noticed. Just as well. He was in the market for a surgeon, not a lover.

"We, meaning everyone at the Castle—aka Paddington's—*obviously* imagine Amira is a gorgeous little girl, and I, for one, can't wait to meet her. So!" Robyn dropped the used wipe into her satchel and clapped her hands onto her knees. "Where is she?"

"I'm sorry?" Idris crossed his legs, leaned back in his chair, all the while locking eyes with her. He was used to conducting interviews. Not the other way around. Who was this woman? Mini-hurricane or a much-needed breath of fresh air?

* * *

"Amira?" Robyn prompted, panicking for a second that she'd walked into the wrong Sheikh's suite in the wrong fancy hotel. All the fripperies and hoo-ha of these places made her nervous. Or was it just the Sheikh? Idris.

He had breathtaking presence. The photo the hospital had supplied with his bio had been flattering—pitch-black eyes, high cheekbones, dark chestnut hair—a tick in all of the right boxes, so that was little wonder. But in real life?

A knee-wobbler.

She only hoped it didn't show. Much.

She tried a discreet sidelong look in his direction but the full power of his dark-eyed gaze threatened a growing impatience.

He had *said he was Idris Al Khalil and not the long-lost son of Omar Sharif, right?*

"Amira," she repeated, unsuccessfully reining her voice back to its normal low octave. "Where did you say your daughter was?"

"Out," came the curt reply.

Huh. Not a flicker of emotion.

Still waters running deep or just a protective papa bear?

Not the way she usually liked to do things, but then she wasn't in the habit of "pitching" herself to be the surgeon of choice, either. One of the few things she solidly knew about herself was that when it came to Ear, Nose and Throat surgeries, she was one of the best. If she thought there was someone else better for the job she wouldn't have even showed up. But this was her gig. She'd known it from the moment she saw Amira's case history.

She tipped her chin upward, eyes narrowing as she watched Idris observe her in return. His black eyes met hers with a near tactile force. Unnerving.

She looked away. Maybe this was some powerful sheikh-type rite of passage she had to go through. She crinkled her nose for a moment before chancing another glance at him.

Yup. Still watching her. Expectantly. Still super-gorgeous.

She pursed her lips. He'd better not be waiting for a song and dance.

She glanced at her watch.

That was about half a second used up, then.

Looked up at the ceiling—eyes catching with his on the way up.

Still staring at her.

She remembered a trick one of her colleagues taught her. Pretend he was in his underwear. She gave him her best measured look all the while feeling her blush deepen as she pictured all six-foot-something of Idris naked, which was really…

much nicer than she probably should be finding the experience.

This whole staring/not staring thing was a bit unnerving. Part of her wished she'd brought a sock puppet.

Robyn! Do not resort to sock puppets!

She clapped her hands onto her knees again.

"So…what do I call you?"

His dark eyebrows drew together into a consternated furrow.

"Idris."

"Oh!" She blinked her surprise. "Phew! I was a bit nervous there that I was meant to bow or 'your highness' you or something. Idris. Great. Beautiful name. I believe that's after one of the Islamic prophets in the Qur'an. Yes? Did you know it's also a Welsh name meaning 'ardent lord' or 'prince'? Fitting, right?"

"I am neither a prophet nor a prince," he answered tightly.

Okay. So he was a king, or a sheikh, or a sheikh king. Whatever. It made no difference to her, not with how full her plate was with the hospital on the brink of closing and an endless list of patients Paddington's could help if only its doors were kept open. Besides—she chewed on her lower lip as she held another untimed staring contest with him—she was just making chitchat until his daughter showed up.

Blink.

He won. Whether or not he knew it. Who could stare at all that…chiseled perfection without blinking? He had it all. The proud cheekbones. The aquiline nose. Deliciously perfect caramel-colored skin. The ever so slightly cleft chin just visible beneath more than a hint of a five o'clock shadow. She didn't know why, but she was almost surprised at his short, immaculately groomed dark hair. He would've suited a mane of the stuff—blowing in the wind as he rode a horse bareback across the dunes. Or whatever it was sheikhs did in their spare time. The color of his hair was run-your-fingers-through-it gorgeous. Espresso-rich. Just…rich. Everything about him screamed privileged. Polar opposites, then.

Of course she'd blinked first.

"Well, you know there's also a mountain in Wales—Idris's Chair. And just look at you there—sitting in a chair." She raised her eyebrows expectantly. Most people would, at the very least, feign a smile.

Nothing.

"It rhymes!" She tacked on with a hopeful grin, trying her best to keep her nerves at bay.

Nothing.

His lips, though clamped tight, were…sensual. She'd already noticed he curved them up or down to great effect. Disconcerting in a man who, on all other counts, embodied the definition of an alpha male. The perfect amount of six-foot-something. For her, anyway. She liked to be able to look a man in the eye without too much chin tilting. If she were in heels? Perfect. Match. Not that she was on the market for a boyfriend or anything. She bit down on the inside of her cheek to stifle a guffaw. As if.

He looked fit. Athletically so. She would've laid money on the fact the hotel swimming pool had seen some well-turned-out laps this morning from the spread of his shoulders filling out what had to be a tailor-made suit. She tipped her chin to the side, finger tapping on her lips, wondering if she could drum up the Arabic word for *tailor*.

"Here we are! I even found a mug! The butler told me builder's tea always has to come in a mug. Preferably with a chip, but I'm afraid this one has no chips."

Robyn lifted her gaze, grateful to see Idris's assistant arrive, face wreathed in a triumphant smile, carrying a tray laden with tea fixings and a huge pile of scrummy-looking biscuits. Were they…? Oh, *wow*. Dark chocolate–covered ginger biscuits. In abundance!

"These are my absolute favorite!"

"We've done our research. Let us hope," Idris continued in his lightly accented English, "that you have done yours."

The words were a dare. One she'd needed no prompting to resist.

"It's actually been fascinating going over Amira's notes. It's kept me up at night." She saw a flash of something indecipherable brighten Idris's dark eyes. "In the best possible way."

Kaisha set the tea tray down between them.

"Heavens! There are enough biscuits here for an army! Is Amira coming with a group of her friends?"

"No. This is just for you," she answered, her beautiful headscarf swishing gently forward as she leaned to pour a cup of mint-scented tea for Idris and herself from a beautiful china teapot.

"Oh, you are a sweetie. Thank you. It's Kaisha, isn't it?" Robyn asked.

"That's right."

Robyn repeated the name. "In Japanese it means enterprising, or enterprise, I think." She found herself looking to Idris for confirmation. He looked like a man who had answers in abundance.

"I thought you said you weren't a linguist, Miss—"

"Doctor," Robyn jumped in with a smile. It was her whole life—her job at Paddington's—and heaven knew she'd far rather be defined by her work than her less edifying home life as a spinster.

"Doctor," Idris corrected, eyebrows lifting as if he were amused by her insistence upon being called by her rightful title. "For someone who professes to only speak 'menu' you seem to know your way around the world's languages."

"Oh, yes, well…" She felt her cheeks grow hot. Again. Not a handy time to have a creamy complexion. She twisted her fingers together, hoping they would help her divine the perfect way to confess just how much of a nerd she was. Nothing sprang to mind so she dove into the pool of true confessions. "I've studied quite a few sign languages from around the world. It comes in handy as an ENT specialist. Many countries share similar signs for the same word, but it's always useful to know the word in the spoken language given we have patients joining us from around the world and a lot of them—as many as I can encourage actually—are lip readers. So—" she signed as she spoke "—that is why I had prepared for meeting Amira and not you."

"I see." Idris's dark-as-night eyes widened and she felt her heart sink. Why, oh, *why* did administration see fit to send her out on these meet-and-greet jobbies? She got too nervous. Talked too much. Way too much. She really would've preferred to meet the child—or patient—as the administrators insisted on calling them, on her own.

Patient. The word gave her shivers. The people who came to them at a time when they were sick, or injured and needing a healing touch—they were all *children*. Children with names and faces, likes and dislikes, and in some cases, the ability to knit the world's longest scarf.

Her fingers crept across the couch and rubbed a bit of the damp wool between her fingers. The gift was as precious to her as if the children she'd never have had made it for her. An ectopic pregnancy had seen to that dream. So her life was filled with countless "adoptees."

Children.

"Patient" sounded so *clinical* and she, along with the rest of the staff at the Castle—as the turreted building had long been nicknamed—wanted the children who came to them to be treated with individual respect and care. With or without the hospital gown, tubes and IVs. Row upon row of medicines, oxygen tanks, tracheal tubes and hearing aids. They were *children* for whom she tried her very best to make the world—or at least Paddington Children's Hospital—a better place to be.

If Amira's records were anything to go by—and Idris was willing to accept the cutting edge treatment she thought her hospital could offer—Robyn knew, with the right team of surgeons, specialists and, annoyingly, *funding*, she could help his little girl hear for the very first time.

So…it was suck it up and woo the Sheikh, help his daughter and save the hospital in the process.

CHAPTER TWO

"LET ME START AGAIN."

Idris's growing impatience won out over the desire to return Robyn's infectious smile. "I wasn't under the impression we had started *anything*, much less the interview I was expecting to conduct."

He knew he was being contrary but this woman unnerved him. Her watchful tigress eyes flicked around the room on a fruitless quest to come up with reasons for his terse response. She wouldn't find what she sought there. In the immaculate soft furnishings and discreet trappings of the über-wealthy. The answer to his coldness stood guard at the surrounds of his heart. Unreachable.

And she would have to do a bit more than smile and catch him off guard to be the one he chose to operate on his daughter.

He was the wall people had to break through to get to Amira. He'd lost one love of his life to the medical "profession." He'd be damned if he lost another.

He shifted in his chair, well aware Robyn was already unwittingly chinking away at some of his

usually impenetrable defenses. This woman—
ray of light, more like—was a near antithesis
to everything his life had been these last seven
years. Where he was wary and overprotective,
she was virtually bursting with life, enthusiasm
and *kindness*.

He didn't think any of the other surgeons had
so much as spoken to Kaisha other than to say
"tea" or "coffee." Perhaps a nod of dismissive
thanks, but in his book, consideration was everything. Particularly in his role as leader of Da'har.
Every decision he made about the small desert
kingdom would, ultimately, affect each citizen.
As such, he took no decision lightly, altered no
laws of the land to benefit one group of people
and not another. Life on this small planet was already unjust enough on its own. He'd learned that
the hard way. And regrouped out of necessity.

The last thing the people of Da'har needed was
a leader drowning in grief at the loss of his wife.
Seven years ago his newborn daughter had needed
a father with purpose. Direction. So he'd shut the
doors on the past and sharply fine-tuned himself
to focus on Amira and the role she would one day
take on as Sheikha of Da'har and all her people.
People whose voices she now longed to hear.

"Where are all the toys?" Robyn asked pointedly.

"I'm sorry?" Idris swung his attention back

toward her, not realizing his thoughts had wandered so far away.

"Toys? You did bring your daughter with you, right? And she's seven so..." He watched her brightly lit eyes scan the immaculate sitting room. "Where does she play?"

"She's at the zoo with Thana."

Kaisha's eyes widened at his words. He knew as well as she, he would normally never tell a virtual stranger his daughter's whereabouts. Or to call him Idris for that matter. He'd offered no such "common" courtesy to the surgeons he'd met before Robyn. Something about her elicited a sense of...comfort. Ease. She exuded warmth. Albeit, a higgledy-piggledy variety of warmth—but she seemed trustworthy, nonetheless. Which was interesting. Trust wasn't something he extended to others when it came to his daughter.

"And Thana is her...?" He bristled at Robyn's open-ended question. He never had to face this sort of questioning in Da'har. Or, generally, anywhere else. His wife's death during childbirth had been international news. Where their wedding had lit up television broadcasts, her funeral had darkened screens around the globe. It was near impossible to explain how leaden his feet had felt as he'd followed her casket, Amira's tiny form tightly swaddled in his arms, the pair of them making their way toward the newly dug grave site. He swallowed the sour sensation that never failed to twist through his gut at the memory.

"Her nanny."

Robyn winced. He could see she remembered now. The myriad expressions her face flashed through and finally landed on was something he recognized too well.

The widowed Sheikh and his deaf daughter...all alone in their grief at the loss of the Sheikha.

So.

He quirked an appraising eyebrow.

She *had* done her research, after all. Just wasn't going to any pains to prove it.

"Right!" Robyn pulled open the flap to her satchel and pulled out a thick sheaf of papers, which she knocked into an exacting rectangle on the glass coffee table. "I generally prefer to do this sort of initial 'meet' with the child. Amira," she corrected. "While I am relatively certain the type of surgery and treatment I am proposing will suit her case, I also like to make sure it suits *her.*"

"What do you mean?" None of the other surgeons seemed to care a jot about Amira's thoughts on the matter. They just wanted to showboat their latest clinical trials...for a price, of course. A large one.

"When someone who is profoundly deaf has hearing restored, it can be quite shocking. Not all deaf people, you may be surprised to learn, *want* to hear."

"That is not the case with Amira."

Robyn gave him a gentle but firm smile before continuing. "It would be *preferable* to hear that from Amira. Sometimes what a parent desires for their child is different from what the child themselves wants. Tell me, how does she communicate?"

"She mostly reads lips, although—" he raised a hand as Robyn's own lips parted to interject "—we have our own sign language of sorts. As I'm sure you are aware, there is not yet a regionally recognized sign language between the Arab nations as there is in America or here in the United Kingdom."

Robyn was nodding along, the tiniest flicker of "been there, done that" betraying the fact he wasn't telling her anything she didn't know already.

"And is her lipreading in Arabic, French and English?"

Hackles rising, Idris checked the volume of his response. "Da'har's local dialect is what interests her most as the people of my kingdom are the ones she will one day be Sheikha to. Though she speaks a smattering of the others as we travel together regularly. Do bear in mind, *Doctor*, she is only seven."

"I have met some very savvy seven-year-olds in my day." Her chin jutted forward decisively.

Was she mocking him? Amira was the most precious thing in his life. He was hardly going to overwhelm his already serious little girl with an endless stream of tutors and languages when life was innately challenging for her.

When his eyes met hers, he was heartened to see Robyn's countenance matched her words. She seemed to have…*respect*…for her patients. He notched up a point for her. A small one. But a point, nonetheless.

"Shame." Robyn was shaking her head, fanning out some of the papers she'd brought. "It's much easier to learn multiple languages as a child. The younger, the better, some say. Particularly if it's not in a scholastic setting." Her eyes made a derisive skid across the decidedly "grown-up" hotel suite.

"Actually…" Kaisha interjected shyly. "Amira's English is pretty good and we have been practicing some British Sign Language. She seems to enjoy it."

"You've not told me this!" Idris knew it wasn't something to be angry about—but why would they keep this from him? A small twinge of concern that his own serious demeanor might be the reason teased at his conscience. Then he dismissed it. He was who he was. A father who put his daughter above everything.

"It was a surprise. For Dr. Kelly." Kaisha jumbled the words together, then launched herself into some fastidious note-taking to avoid any reaction Idris might have.

"That's excellent!" Robyn gave a fingertip pitter-patter clap.

"British Sign Language is closer to French—so if she takes that up as well, it sounds as though she's got some solid grounding in the wonderful world of the polyglot!"

Kaisha beamed with pride.

"Hold on!" Idris unsuccessfully tried to rein in the women's enthusiasm. "What has all of this got to do with the operation to restore her hearing?"

"Everything," Robyn replied solidly.

"And why is that?" Idris asked, now feeling sorely tested.

"Because there is always the chance it might not work."

A thick silence settled between them as he took on board what none of the other surgeons dared suggest. Failure. It was a courageous thing to admit.

"I thought you were one of the best."

"I am," Robyn replied without so much as a blink of an eye. "But Amira's case is a tricky one and the treatment I'm proposing has never been done in exactly this way. Not to mention, I've never done it in tandem with gene therapy."

"Gene therapy?" Idris's hackles went straight up. It sounded invasive. Dangerously so.

"Don't worry…don't worry." Robyn waved away his concerns as if they were minor. "This is really exciting stuff. During my time in Boston Pediatrics—"

"I thought you were based at Paddington's."

Was *nothing* as it seemed with this woman?

"I am," she confirmed patiently, then gave a self-effacing laugh. "Unlike most of the human race I like to take my 'holidays' at other hospitals. See what my fellow comrades in the Ear, Nose and Throat world are up to."

"So…you *work* on holiday." It came out as a statement.

"I never feel like I'm at work," she replied, looking shocked he could think otherwise. "I love what I do. So, really, I'm living the dream!"

Idris saw something just then—the tiniest of winces as she spoke of her "perfect life."

That she was passionate about medicine he had no doubt. But there was something missing, something personal. Which was what she seemed to be making this whole affair by the constant reminders that Amira wasn't available for "inspection."

He gave a dissatisfied grunt at the thought, smoothing away an invisible crease on his trousers.

Work and play might be one and the same for Robyn, but he had yet to get a handle on what it was she was actually going to *do* for his daughter apart from test her emotional elasticity. What was she expecting? A picket fence lifestyle for a girl who had lost her mother at birth and would one day rule a nation, all the while coping with profound deafness?

If she could handle that with the grace and charm she exhibited on a daily basis, Amira would certainly be able to handle…

Ah…

Idris put two and two together, suddenly seeing the sense behind everything Robyn—*Dr. Kelly*—was saying. One devastating loss was big enough. Something she would have to live with forever. The second? Her dream of being able to hear the voices of the people she would one day serve as leader?

He glanced at his watch, wondering how long it would take to bring Amira back from the zoo. Then again, he still hadn't heard Robyn's surgical plans. He was hardly going to give her hope before he'd heard Dr. Sunshine's proposal.

"Okay, Idris—Your Highness. This is the part for focusing." Robyn's entire body looked as though it were ready to spring from the sofa as she spoke. "I am particularly excited about the different components of this surgery. I think Amira—when I eventually meet her—will be pretty interested to learn she'll be one of the first children to receive a 3-D printout of not one but two inner ear bones. The stapes or stirrup, and the incus—or anvil as it is commonly known. I'm guessing you're relatively *au fait* with this terminology, right?" She didn't pause for an answer, just a quick glance in his direction as she pushed a couple of maps of an ear in his direction highlighting the work she proposed to do. Then, from her seemingly bottomless pit of a satchel, she pulled out a large model of an ear.

"This was more for Amira's sake, but as she's not here, you'll do."

"How very kind," Idris answered dryly. Whether or not Robyn took any notice of his tone was beyond him as she was utterly engrossed in taking apart the pieces of the gigantic model to reveal a beautiful side view of the intricately constructed organ.

"As she was born prematurely, it looks as though a couple of Amira's middle ear bones had some trouble developing completely, leading to the conductive hearing loss and—for whatever reason, it could be her diet, could be all the other factors a preemie has to go through—her body hasn't quite caught up with the development she should have gone through by this point. It's also apparent that the sensory hairs in her ear were damaged at some point. It could have been in the gestational period, but I think it is more likely it was during the labor. Sometimes the use of medicines that are beneficial to the mother can affect the baby—"

"Stop there. I've heard enough."

Idris clenched his teeth, feeling the telltale twitch in his jaw as he did. No one had so much as dared to suggest Amira's hearing loss had been caused by the medical treatment his wife had received. He'd never hold his wife's fight for survival accountable for his daughter's condition. At first he'd thought it had been punishment for being too happy. A beautiful wife, a nation who adored the pair of them, a child on the way... The lightning strikes of how cruel life could actually be had been blunt and unforgiving.

Robyn leaned forward and reached out a hand, taking one of Idris's in her own. His instinct was to yank his hand away. It had been years since he'd known the comforting touch of a woman. Years since he'd thought such a thing would ever be possible after he'd lost his beloved wife. If Robyn noticed, nothing in her expression betrayed the fact.

"This is a big step," she began, the warmth

of her fingers beginning to mesh with his own. "For you *and* your daughter. I would rather call the entire thing off if you feel it's too iffy. There is always the option of cochlear implants or bone conducting hearing aids. They do offer excellent opportunities for many hearing-impaired children, but given the damage to Amira's sensory hairs, I believe they'll offer minimal aid in your daughter's case. If you like I can show you the details for the other surgeries."

"No need." Idris extracted his hand from hers and stood, suddenly impatient to get things under way. His own fears, his need to control the situation, would have to be controlled. For Amira's sake. Putting all of his faith in a surgeon for his daughter's well-being terrified him, but something about Robyn told him she would do everything in her power to do what she could for Amira.

"We will do the surgery, as you prescribed, but on one condition."

"Oh! I…uh…" She threw a look over each shoulder as if expecting the condition to appear from behind the sofa.

Idris bit back a smile. She was clearly a doctor, through and through. A negotiator? Not so much. Children seemed to be the medium through which she communicated with the rest of the world. Adults, less comfortable terrain. Or was it just him that made her squirm? A flash of sexual prowess shot through him. Fleeting—powerful enough to leave aftershocks.

"What exactly is this condition?" Robyn shot him a wary look when a giraffe didn't pop up behind her. "I don't dance, sing or play poker if any of those are your poison."

"You will come to Da'har."

Her eyebrows shot up and her mouth popped into a pretty O as she took on board his proposal. She wanted him out of his comfort zone...and it looked as though his request meant she would have to leave hers.

Why?

"To spend time with Amira, of course. As you requested," he couldn't resist adding.

Robyn jumped to her feet, raising her hands in protest.

"There's no need for me to leave the hallowed shores of Blighty to do my best in surgery." Her eyes zigzagged between him and Kaisha as if trying to divine a hidden meaning in the request. Demand? Even he wasn't sure. What he did know was if he was going to acquiesce to her demands she'd better be prepared to meet him halfway. Putting his daughter's future in the hands of virtual stranger? Not an option.

"When we're in Da'har—"

"Oh, my goodness me! Let's not count our

camels before they hatch!" Robyn laughed nervously, faltered, regrouped, then put on what he suspected was a self-taught stern expression as she wagged a finger at him. "I don't exactly remember saying I would come along. I am the head of surgery at a very busy hospital that—"

"Is under threat of closure and relocation outside of London? Riverside, I believe the new site is called?" he finished coolly.

He was no game player, but if Paddington Children's Hospital was on the brink of an unwanted closure, he had the means to change that. His pockets were deep. Very deep. But his daughter's welfare came first. The thought of losing Amira under any circumstances chilled him to his very marrow. Something just as deep-seated told him Robyn was the woman to perform Amira's surgery, but only after a few more boxes had been ticked. "You will come to Da'har to allay my concerns—"

"Concerns?"

A piercing shot of anger coursed through Idris that she could even dare to suggest he would feel otherwise.

"Yes. Concerns. Shall I spell it out for you? A *father's* concerns. Surely, Dr. Kelly, you are not unfamiliar with the love a parent has for a child?"

Robyn went deathly still. She blinked, hiding behind her eyelids a look of pure, unadulterated grief. When she opened them again, her eyes bore little of the light they'd shone with earlier and Idris knew he was at fault for unearthing a deep sorrow. A hollow victory if ever there was one.

"I will have to talk to the board," she said. "Ensure appropriate replacements can be made…"

"Good." He gave a curt nod, his tone back to its usual brusque efficiency. It wasn't as if he could comfort her. Pull her into his arms and tell her whatever it was that had thrown a shadow over her sunlit eyes would one day be better. He was proof that time was not a healer of all wounds.

"Right. Very well, then. When shall we book your flight? Or, if you care to join us, we will be taking the jet back. Is it tomorrow afternoon, Kaisha? Amira's booked in to see a premiere of some sort tonight—a musical—otherwise we'd be off today."

"You're going to see *Princesses and Frogs*?" Robyn shoved her dark thoughts away, grateful for the distraction. The highly anticipated musical had been sold out for months and months. She'd been hoping to bring some of her friends from the hospital…well, patients, but they always ended up finding a way into her heart no matter how "doctory" she tried to be.

"Yes. Very nice seats, I'm led to believe. Would you care to join us?"

Robyn barked out an ungainly laugh. "I doubt you'd be able to get extra tickets at this point."

"It won't be a problem. We always book out the Royal Dress Circle."

She cringed as Idris caught her raised eyebrows, even more embarrassed at her reaction to the show of wealth when he finished, "In case Amira would like to bring along a friend or two. As you speak British Sign Language, you could be useful if she needs some additional interpreting along the way. Is there anyone else you'd like to invite along?" She felt his eyes traveling down to her bare ring finger and protectively covered her left hand with her right.

She fidgeted for a minute under his cool gaze, then crossed her arms, in a B-grade show of giving his question a few moments' consideration. Idris didn't need to know she was a dedicated singleton. One whose daily torture and pleasure it was to enter Paddington's and spend day after day surrounded by children knowing she would never have one of her own. Lacerating her heart by getting close to yet another young patient was always a risk. One she'd have to take if it meant saving the hospital that had saved her in her darkest days. Her hands, as they always did, crept down to protect the area where she would have carried a child if things had gone differently. If life had been kind. She blinked. Kind.

Idris hadn't known much kindness at the hands of Mother Nature, either.

"It would be great if I could come along…to meet Amira." Her brow crinkled as she continued. "In the light of which, I really don't think it's necessary to take up your time and resources to go to Da'har."

"Nonsense. Expense is the least of my problems." Idris tutted, crossing to the sofa where Robyn was sitting. She watched, wordlessly, as he picked up the crumpled ball that was her raincoat and shook it out. The scarf one of "her" kids had given her fell to the ground. When she bent to pick it up, she conked heads, rather impressively, with Idris.

They rose simultaneously, hands clamped on foreheads. As comedy moments went…this was up there. Except neither of them were laughing.

His eyes…those *beautiful* near black eyes of his held on to hers as if they were speaking to each other. A silent conversation winging its way, effortlessly, to her very core where she was feeling rather heated and a little bit…*giddy.*

Da'har was *meant to be nice this time of year.*

Idris regrouped more quickly than Robyn and all she could do was watch his lips as he spoke.

"If you need a few days to rearrange your schedule…" She watched as his Adam's apple dipped and resurfaced. Was he feeling it, too?

"I'm quite sure the hospital administration will be…flexible…about your hospital duties when they understand the complexities surrounding your upcoming surgery."

"It's not the surgery I'm worried about." Her fingers flew to cover her lips. *Gulp.* She was really going to have to curtail her out-loud voice.

"Dr. Kelly, I'm not certain how much your administrative team has told you about me, but in order for this surgery to go ahead I'm afraid there are a few hurdles to leap. My daughter is my utmost priority and as much as you want to understand Amira, I need to understand you."

"Oh, no, no. I don't go under the microscope." *Not a chance.* No one—no matter how sexy, powerful and unnervingly sensual they were—no one opened up her private life for inspection. Case. Closed. She dug her trainers into the thick carpet and gave a shake of the head, wishing she'd commandeered her wild spray of curls into some sort of obedience. "Nonnegotiable."

"My daughter, my rule book."

"Ha! Wow." Despite her best efforts to stem her response, she snorted. "Someone's a little used to getting what he wants."

He quirked an eyebrow in response; a ribbon of heat flickered through her belly as she watched his lips part to respond to her, a full octave lower than usual.

"And someone's going to have to learn to be a bit more flexible to get what she wants."

Robyn could've sworn she saw the hint of a smile on his lips before he continued briskly. "You will, of course, need to meet the team you will work with for the surgery in Da'har before I allow it—"

"Allow it?" *Sorry, pal.* Sheikh or no sheikh, she and she alone decided whether or not the surgery was green-lit.

"Yes. Allow it," Idris replied, entirely unaffected by her interior monologue. "I make decisions about Amira and no one else. It's the job of a parent to protect, is it not?"

Robyn bit down hard enough on the inside of her cheek to draw blood as he continued. She'd never be a parent and, as such, was denied any right of reply. This time her silence drew venom.

"How else do you recommend I look after my daughter's welfare?" Idris snapped. He would move heaven and earth for Amira. Retaining control of her medical treatment was paramount. If he had control, he could ensure nothing would happen to her. Loss—the aching, hollowed-out-heart kind of grief he had felt when his wife had died—was not something he would ever go through again. He pressed his lips tightly together as Robyn began, again, to fight her corner.

"By trusting me and the other physicians at Paddington's to do our very best—as we always do," she replied, only just managing to keep the bite out of her own voice. Kaisha, Idris noticed, was inching her way out of the room.

"Then you will do your very best in Da'har."

"Oh, no, no, no." Robyn's index finger went into overdrive. "Not for the surgery. That will happen here." She pointed in the general direction of Paddington's, wagging her finger as if that were the decision maker. "It's Paddington's *world-class facilities*…or nowhere."

The air crackled between them and for just a moment Idris saw a strength in her he doubted few people were privy to. A confidence in her abilities—under her terms—to which he was going to have to acquiesce.

Interesting.

What was it that made Robyn tick? Gave her the strength to disagree with him when everyone else was busy falling over themselves to appease. What would it be like to share the responsibility of Amira's care with someone he trusted? The thought instantly brought him back to his senses. He had no one. Amira's care was his and his alone.

"I can get you anything or anyone you like to work with in Da'har. What does it matter where the surgery takes place?"

"Everything!"

They both froze. Idris felt his features recompose themselves into the unreadable mask he'd worn for so long while the tiniest of twitches on Robyn's face betrayed a fight against the unwelcome sting of tears. His chest tightened. Yes, he wanted control—but not on these terms.

"Isn't a surgical theater the same anywhere?"

Robyn shook her head, clearly not yet trusting herself to speak.

"My daughter's welfare is paramount. She is happiest in Da'har."

"My patient's welfare is paramount and, as such, *I* am happiest operating at Paddington's."

"Tell me, what's so special about it?"

His softer tone suggested a change of tack. One Robyn felt herself drawn to. Even so, she didn't share. Not even her colleagues knew about the ectopic pregnancy that had ended her dreams of having a family of her own. All they knew was that Robyn poured her heart and soul into Paddington's and was as much a part of the place as the very bricks and mortar.

"Spend time in Da'har with us." A smile— one he should use more frequently—accompanied Idris's words. "If you meet my terms, I will meet yours."

"You mean the operation will be at Paddington's?"

"So long as you join us in Da'har. The sooner, the better."

A trip to Da'har.

Her lungs strained against the thought. Even so…something told her this was a throw-caution-to-the-winds moment. It was not like she was facing a life or death decision. What harm could seeing a children's musical and a couple of days in Da'har do in the greater scheme of things apart from scare her witless by yanking her straight out of her comfort zone?

So she'd have a handful of days not knowing if she was coming or going. Days that could change the face of things at Paddington's, making every moment of scrutinizing looks from the desert kingdom's leader worth it.

Idris's eyes bore down on her as he waited for an answer, a shift of his jawline betraying his impatience.

Her tummy flipped.

And…breathe.

See? Survived the first step.

Robyn gave a quick nod and stuck out her hand in as businesslike a fashion as she could muster. "I trust there will be chocolate-covered ginger biscuits where we're going?"

Maybe not quite as grown-up as she'd been aiming for.

"More than enough." Idris's voice deepened as he mirrored her nod, engulfing her hand in both of his as he did. Why hadn't she noticed how large his hands were before? And how *strong*. And gentle enough in their strength to make her feel...*delicate*.

Crikey. If only she could take a pile of those ginger biscuits back with her and curl up in a corner until every last crumb of them had disappeared. A sugar high might be the only way she'd have the strength to go through with this harebrained scheme.

"Kaisha," Idris called over his shoulder, hands still encasing hers as if they were precious jewels, "can we get the rest of Dr. Kelly's biscuits put in a basket or something so that she can bring them back to the hospital. To *share*." He arched an eyebrow at her, all but proving he'd read her mind.

A few moments later, a flame-faced Robyn was jabbing at the lift buttons, a wicker basket swinging from her arm laden with enough ginger biscuits to feed an army.

C'mon, c'mon, c'mon! Where was the elite and exclusive service when you needed it? She could feel the Sheikh's bodyguards train their eyes on her, hoping they read nothing into the jiggling she could feel beginning as a hit of nerves overtook her entire upper body.

He'd seen into her *soul*.

How was that even possible? Less than an hour with Idris—Sheikh Idris Al Khalil. Her polar opposite if ever there was one, and yet…

She shot a glance over her shoulder again and grimaced. If the muscle men evaporated she could start banging her head against the controls hoping to knock some sense into herself at the same time. What on earth was she doing? Agreeing to up stakes and hang out in a desert kingdom with the cool-as-a-cucumber mind reader? Her private life was exactly that and she didn't know how many more X-ray vision looks she could deflect.

A low groan filled the space around her. A droning moan of despair. Oh, wait. *She* was making that sound. Oops.

She turned around and flashed the bodyguards a quick smile, which grew brighter when she heard the lift ping and the doors click-clack open.

The sooner she could get back into the comforting surrounds of Paddington's, the better.

CHAPTER THREE

"HE SAID *WHAT* EXACTLY?"

Robyn scanned the sea of expectant expressions, wishing she weren't the center of attention. Limelight and Robyn were not a good combination. But these people were her friends as well as her colleagues. The surgeons and doctors who were pouring their hearts, minds and endless energies into keeping the doors of Paddington Children's Hospital open.

"Well, Dominic, um…" *Why did they send me?* "Biscuit, anyone?" She pushed the basket of sweets to the middle of the surgical ward's central desk and forced on what she hoped was a winning smile.

"Claire said *you* said *he* said you'd have to go to Da'har."

"Hold on a minute, Alistair. You know how I feel about riding the gossip train." She tsked, then gulped as the sea of expectant faces grew more impatient.

"For heaven's sake, Robyn! I'm not engaging in idle gossip, I'm trying to learn if there is even the smallest sliver of a chance we can save Paddington's from this ridiculous move out to Riverside!"

"You know, you have a lovely voice, Alistair. Is that what drew you to him, Claire? The voice?" The more the group stared at her, the more tongue-tied she became. "Can't I just send out a memo or something?"

Rosie Hobbes—still glowing from her recent engagement to Dr. Marchetti—turned her flame-haired bob and made another stab at extracting information from Robyn. "You don't need to give us a blow-by-blow account of what happened with His Excellency, but the key details would be useful."

"You mean Idris?" Robyn crinkled her nose. Rosie's fiancé was, after all, a duke and no one went around calling *him* His Excellency.

A general *"ooh"* that said, *Look who's on first-name terms with the Sheikh*, circled Robyn like an ever-tightening snare.

"Just because most of you lot got swept away with spring fever and are all loved up doesn't mean I can't carry on with a *professional* relationship!" She could've added in a bit about the pregnancy chair having done far too much work this year, but no need to turn herself into a human voodoo doll. Wide eyes continued to stare expectantly. Provocatively. Annoyingly.

"It's August. Cupid's month off. I have it on good authority."

"Methinks the lady doth protest too much," Alistair teased, giving his fiancée, Claire, a little nuzzle as he did.

It wasn't as if Idris was all gorgeous and irresistibly off-limits or anything.

"If you're on a first-name basis," Rosie chimed in, "he's obviously keen for you to do the surgery."

"He is," she conceded. "But when I told him I would only do the surgery here at the Castle, Idris said he would only agree if I went to Da'har."

His name felt both foreign and familiar when she spoke it. A sweetness upon her tongue. Not a sensation to get used to. "Besides, a first-name basis doesn't mean I have to fly out and see his magical desert kingdom by moonlight, okay?"

Maybe Alistair had a point.

"Robyn!" Rosie persisted. "You don't want to move out to the business park of so-called 'Riverside' any more than the rest of us do. Paddington's must stay open. We just want to know if there's anything we can do to help you."

Apart from dropping the playground teasing about Idris, nothing sprang to mind. This was solidly on her shoulders. Unfortunately.

"No, not really. I should probably speak with Victoria about his proposal."

"Your chic Sheikh has asked you to marry him?" Matthew teased, receiving a jab in the ribs from Claire as Robyn's mouth screwed up into an *"eww"* face.

"Is it possible that he's not a chic sheikh?" Rosie asked with false innocence.

"Or that he's not really a sheikh?" Victoria posited, another biscuit disappearing from the ever-diminishing pile.

"Maybe the chic Sheikh already has five wives and our Robyn really deserves to be wife number one."

There was a collective nod of heads.

"Get your heads out of the registry office! The lot of you!"

Too cranky.

She opened her mouth to fix the mood-change grenade she'd tossed into the midst of the group, gaped like a fish for a moment, then dove in. "He obviously loved his late wife very much and from his…less than warm demeanor, I can happily inform you he will be bending his knee and asking me to marry him in—oh, just about never." She grabbed a biscuit and ran her finger along the edge before looking up at her peers. "And don't look so surprised!"

Marriage had been on the cards once, but after her epic fail in the baby-making department?

Never again. She needed to contain the situation. Set them straight.

"Don't make fun of my chic Sheikh."

The eyes trained on her collectively widened.

That probably wasn't the best way to handle it, Robyn.

"Gah!" Robyn cried, zigzagging her index finger around the group with her stern expression on full tilt. "All of you are very, *very* silly."

And she would miss them heart and soul if the hospital were to close. Which only meant one thing.

She'd need to buy a suitcase.

She shushed their teasings and proddings, then put on her I'm-the-head-of-department face.

"Idris wants me to go to Da'har for a few days to get to know his daughter better." She looked around the group to garner support that she shouldn't leave Paddington's.

"So go!" Dominic urged. "I'm pretty certain I speak for Victoria when I say this. If it'll help Paddington's—*go.*"

"Dominic," she pleaded, "this is your bag, not mine. I'm bound to make an idiot out of myself or put my foot in it."

"Is not going worth compromising the Castle's future?" Alistair's question hushed the group collectively.

"Not fair! You all know how much this place

means to me." Paddington's was her heartbeat. Her lifesaver. The job offer to work here had come the same week she'd had her insides removed and her relationship had imploded. It had literally pulled her out of the dark and into a new world of possibility. Of hope that, even though she would never be a mother, she could dedicate her life to helping other women's children survive. Thirteen years later she was still here—but soon Paddington's might not be.

Her eyes moved from surgeon to doctor to paramedic to nurse. Each of them an unwitting role-player in her fight to survive her darkest days. She brightened as an idea struck. "Why don't *you* go to Da'har, Dominic? I already said I'd go to the theater with him. I'll meet Amira there. I'm sure we'll hit it off just fine and then, once the show's over, I'll let His Excellency know it'll be you and not me who'll be joining him in Da'har."

"What?" Rebecca barked through a mouthful of ginger biscuit. "You're going on a sheikh date?"

"Yeah, right. Just like the genie is going to pop out of the bottle and make all my wishes come true when I—uh—rub it."

"Hold on a minute." Dominic raised his hand before giving Robyn's shoulder a gentle rub. "As fun as all of this is, Robyn, you are the Castle's head of surgery, not to mention the doctor who would be performing Amira's treatment. You should not only be going to the theater on your sheikh date, but you should be preparing yourself to eat dates with the Sheikh from afar in Da'har."

"I thought you said we were done rhyming." Robyn grabbed a biscuit and took a defiant chomp. Hopefully it would help mask the jitters launching a Mach-force invasion on her nervous system.

"We are. And you are done prevaricating. Get out the Factor Fifty, my friend. You're going to Da'har." Dominic grinned.

She widened her eyes to appeal to her fellow surgeons. "Being in the operating theater? Piece of cake. I've already thought of an amazing team, and on the cab ride back I checked with one of the specialists at Boston, and he's already looking into flights. It would take his research global. The whole publicity thing? That's your terrain, Dom. You're the one who can get it all over TV."

"And you're the one who can do the surgery that will get Paddington's the right kind of press. But *only if* you go to Da'har and win over the Sheikh!" He finished with a persuasive smile all the while fixing her with his bright blue eyes, and for just a moment she could see why Victoria had fallen for him. Not that she thought of anyone, ever, in that way anymore. Except that a certain pair of inky black eyes flashed into her mental cinema. She blinked them away, forcing herself to focus on the words coming out of Dominic's mouth.

"We can clear your schedule from tomorrow—" He raised a hand to stop Robyn from interjecting, proving just how right she had been to put him at the helm of the PR campaign to save the hospital from closure. He flopped an arm around her shoulders as she squirmed beneath the imploring gazes of her colleagues.

She was great with children and in surgery. Being the object of everyone's undivided attention was—

"Oops—easy there, Ryan!" She lurched out from underneath Dominic's arm to steady the young boy as he tried out his new crutches along the hospital corridors. "Big step up from the wheelchair, eh?"

Ryan beamed up at her, too focused on staying upright to answer back. The seven-year-old had come such a long way from when he'd first been brought in after the horrible primary school fire. He was one of dozens of children now recovering in leaps and bounds because of the help they received here at Paddington's. Help they might not be able to get if she didn't get over herself and board a plane to a place she'd barely heard of let alone was familiar with.

She turned back to the cluster of colleagues awaiting her response. "Fine." She shook her head with a sigh and a halfhearted smile. "You win. I'll go."

A smattering of applause followed her as she grabbed another biscuit and offered Ryan gentle encouragement as he made his way back along the corridor to his room. If he could fight the odds, so could she.

Idris tapped his foot impatiently. Where *was* she? Kaisha, at his request, had rung the hospital to confirm Robyn was coming and had given her the times.

"You said we'd be in the royal circle, didn't you?"

"Yes. I made it clear she was to tell security she was to be allowed through to our section."

As if she'd need it.

"You said seven-thirty, didn't you?"

"Yes. Three times," Kaisha replied neutrally, fingers skidding along her tablet to check the confirmation email that had accompanied the phone call.

It was at moments like this that Idris was a little surprised Kaisha didn't hand in her notice or tell him to put a sock in it. He was hardly a bundle of laughs at the best of times and this was about the tenth time today he'd been insufferable. Not that he was keeping track or anything; it was just…there'd been a shift today. A shift in the currents of his life, as if things were changing course. He had little doubt what shape the change had come in—blond hair, amber eyes…

Change or no, Kaisha shouldn't be the one to take his discord in the neck.

He signaled for her to put her tablet away.

"Stop. Don't worry. The curtain goes up in a minute or two—just…"

Just what? Go out into the whole of London and find her? Bring the production to a halt while they waited? One meeting and she'd already threaded herself into his psyche—a single gold thread in a tapestry of too much unhappiness.

He cleared his throat and reenergized his tapping. Golden presence or otherwise, the woman was late. He wasn't unaware the fault could be his own. It was very possible he'd been too harsh. Shaping his own fears into too acute a display of anger.

He leaned across to Amira and dropped a kiss on top of her curtain of ebony hair as she diligently worked her way through the program, her index finger distractedly fiddling with a loose tooth. He fought the urge to tell her to leave it be. His parents had allowed him free rein to be a child and he owed it to his daughter to do the same. She would bear full responsibility for ruling Da'har one day. For now? She could worry about her loose tooth.

Amira turned to him and pressed one of her small hands onto his knee, mouthing and signing, "Daddy! You're jiggling the entire balcony!"

"I'm sorry, darling. Just excited for the princesses. Aren't you?"

"Of course," she signed, her brows knitting together as she did. "Do you think there will be dancing frogs?" Her fingers lifted and twirled upon her palm as if it were the stage and her fingers the dancers.

"I can't see why not." He gave what he hoped looked like an enthusiastic nod.

Dancing frogs! Definitely not his *milieu*, but if it lit up his daughter's somber expression, then so much the better.

He looked up sharply as the lights began to dim and the initial glimmerings of the musicians warming up drew to a halt in the orchestra pit. He felt his daughter's eyes on him as he responded to the sound of the trill of a flute, a few seesawed notes upon a violin, the rich scales running along the length of a cello, and his heart ached for her. Ached for the day when she would be able to hear what he did. Music. It had played such a huge part in his life before Amira's mother died. The foundation of so many moments. And when the doctors had told him they had lost her, along with his wife's beautiful smile went his passion for singing.

Some murmuring to his right caught his attention. His security staff were—were they laughing with someone? A flash of bright blond curly hair answered how such a thing was possible.

Robyn Kelly.

Like a bright, energetic force of nature—springtime in human form—she entered the area prepared for Idris and his daughter. He felt himself pluck at his suit's lapels, then run a hand through hair he knew didn't need revamping. *Primping!* His facial features tightened at the thought. She was here to impress them. Not the other way around.

Robyn was walking backward, still laughing at something one of the security guards had said, and when she turned around he was struck, just as dramatically as he had been the first time, by the rich amber luster of her eyes. If she hadn't collided with one of the seats and stumbled, he would have likened her to Persephone. But the Greek goddess had turns of darkness which could turn the world cold and decayed. There didn't seem to be anything that wouldn't flourish underneath the warmth of Robyn's smile.

Curiosity struck as she looked up with an embarrassed smile and inched her way along the row of seats toward him. All too quickly he saw the hidden sadness he'd unearthed earlier when her eyes lit upon Amira and then moved to him. A darkness only she was privy to. And, as their eyes met again when she approached him with a mouthed apology for her lateness, he knew in his heart it was true. There were depths to this woman—hidden sorrows she bore on her own without malice or fury in the way his own grief often manifested itself.

A hint of rain and fresh flowers wafted toward him as she settled into her chair, unlooping the strap of her satchel from around her neck. She scanned the location and again, as an expectant hush filled the theater, mouthed how impressed she was by the seats. She then leaned forward and gave a little wave to Amira.

He watched, mesmerized, as his daughter… *smiled.*

What was it about Robyn that brought about such open joy?

His eyes were locked on Robyn's fingers as she introduced herself to Amira—speaking in Arabic first, then the same again in English.

"Robyn," her slender fingers spelled.

"Like the bird?" his daughter asked, eyes clearly glued on Robyn's lips, her tiny fingers mimicking the Arabic sign for *bird*.

"Very close," Robyn deftly signed back. "Shall we use that as my name?"

Idris's eyes flicked between the two—leaning across his lap as if he weren't there, barely cognizant of the curtain lifting above the stage as Amira and this mystery of a surgeon in Mary Poppins mode decided Robyn's sign language name would be that of little bird.

It suited her.

Robyn's fingers continued signing at lightning speed, mouthing the words as she did that they'd carry on the discussion later and come up with a suitable name for Amira during the interval. In the meantime, she drew their collective attention to the warm wash of light and sequined princesses filling the stage—it was time for fairy tales.

As Idris settled back against the seat, he caught himself smiling. It was fairly clear in this particular scenario who was playing the frog.

"May I sit here?" Amira's dark eyes were huge and hopeful.

Robyn watched Idris's face for a reaction.

Who could say no to *that* face?

Not to mention the wash of relief she felt when the seven-year-old pointed at the seat where Idris had been sitting before the interval.

"It is fine with me." She nodded. Hopefully not too eagerly.

Amira's happy smile was such a reward she

had to freeze her own grin for a moment, hoping to mask a jab of concern. A shift in the "seating plan" was a double-edged sword. The second her eyes had lit upon the gorgeous little girl, Robyn's heart had swooped up and cinched tight. An instant connection. And she knew where that could so easily lead. No matter how often she tried to view children as *work*, they always ended up becoming so much more. The number of times she'd opened up the door to her heart only to suffer the excruciating pain of loss…

It was nothing more than a parent would feel. Of course. And that thought alone threatened to blind her for an instant, sorrow eclipsing pragmatism with the knowledge that she would never be a mother herself. Never have the right to love a child as much as she so often did.

She shook her head clear. She'd promised Victoria she would come see the musical as per Idris's request. All part of the deal to save the hospital. It wasn't personal. It wasn't a reminder she'd never have a child of her own. It was a moment to *savor*.

Little-girl-heaven moments, she called them at Paddington's. This was just an out-of-context meeting made more pronounced by the gilt-edged theater, the front row royal balcony seats, the amazing musical and a certain dark-haired, glowering sheikh begrudgingly shifting over a seat so his daughter could sit next to the British interloper.

She grinned as Amira plopped down with a satisfied nod—the female version of her father. Big brown eyes. A black sheet of polished ebony hair. A heart-shaped face and a near permanent expression of earnest intent on her face.

Amira's beauty was hardly a surprise given the gene pool she'd sprung from. Not that Robyn thought Idris was gorgeous or anything… It was just a question of science and personal preference. Just a little. *Okay, a whole lot.* But she had, on her lightning-fast internet search on the way to the theater, also seen how very much in love he'd been with his late wife—another beauty. It explained the imperiously arched eyebrows and pursed lips when he looked at her—a discombobulated mishmash of science and too much heart on her sleeve.

"So what did you decide upon?"

"Sorry?" Robyn looked up to Idris.

"Amira's sign language name."

"Oh!" Robyn leaned forward so that Amira could see her lips, as well, and began signing. "We forgot, didn't we? What would you like your name to be?"

"I want you to pick it," Amira replied somberly.

"Me?"

When Robyn glanced across at Idris, she saw his eyebrows were raised as high as hers felt.

"Maybe we should wait."

"But what if I don't see you again?"

This time she could practically feel Idris's gaze burning into her—expectant. She hadn't exactly given him an answer, had she?

Victoria's words rang in her head again. "We can delay your surgeries, but we can't put off saving Paddington's. We're down to the wire. He may be our last chance." Then she'd added the line that always spurred Robyn into action. "Just think of all this could do for the children."

Unable to meet Idris's questioning gaze, she shifted in her seat, putting her full focus on Amira.

"What do you say we pick the perfect name another time?"

Amira's shoulders slumped a little, while in the corner of her eye she saw Idris's stiffen.

"When I come to Da'har," Robyn amended, not daring to look toward Idris.

She was certain there would be a look of triumph in those dark eyes of his if she met his gaze now. Unwitting or no, he had found her weak spot. The challenge of a parent to even attempt to love their child as much as they did. Their own flesh and blood. How could she, a barren spinster, ever understand what it meant to love a child?

It was possible. Robyn had felt the deep love again and again. Experienced the pain of loss as many times. And would have to bury her pain if she were to save Paddington's.

Amira looked up at her father, face alight with happy disbelief. As the lights began to lower she swung her head first to Robyn, then to Idris and back again in taut anticipation of the second act.

How to improve upon dancing frogs and swirling princesses? Robyn could hardly stop a giggle from burbling forth. Amira's excitement was contagious.

She had to fight the urge to reach across and hold hands with the little girl, settling on folding her hands in her lap like a reserved nun.

She tsked herself.

If she'd been by Ryan's bedside, the poor lad back at Paddington's who had well and truly captured her heart, she would definitely have taken hold of his hand without hesitation. Or Penelope Craig, with whom she'd spent countless hours reading and rereading the childhood classics. Princesses in attics. Wannabe ballerinas. Discovering magic gardens. She followed Amira's bright eyes as the little girl pushed forward in her seat and leaned against the red velvet balcony ledge to take in the spectacle unfolding in front of them. So...alive! This little girl deserved, at the very least, a shot at having her hearing restored.

So what was making going to Da'har so *difficult*?

When she saw a large hand protectively rub across his daughter's shoulders, she knew the answer instantly.

Idris.

He'd made an impact and it was unsettling her. The man obviously adored his daughter, but his cool reserve felt...not judgy, but...

Critical.

As though each and every thing she did were under a microscope. It made her all squirmy and un-surgeon-like. Well, tough. This was *her* surgery. *Her* terms. Except, of course, for the parts that were his terms. Rearrange her plans, her surgeries, fly thousands of miles away from her life here and—

A sudden change in the orchestra's music caught her attention. Lots of minor chords and eerie lighting filled the theater as the evil Frog King took his long-legged, menacing strides across the stage toward the beautiful fairy princess, bravely facing the man—frog!—who could change everything with the flick of a—

Before she knew what was happening, Amira had clambered into her lap, eyes still glued to the stage, her little hands reaching for Robyn's so she could be wrapped in the safety of her arms.

Instinct took over. Her arms slipped around

Amira's waist, a delicious wash of little-girl aroma filling her senses and she looked to Idris for—what exactly? Approval?

His expression was unreadable. And fleeting. She caught a slight twitch in his jaw as he turned back to the musical as if his daughter was always crawling onto the laps of virtual strangers for a cuddle.

Too much too soon. The vibe was coming off him loud and clear.

Only one way to solve that problem.

She scooped up Amira and handed her toward Idris. His eyes widened, and ever so slightly his implacable expression softened as he reached out his arms and took his daughter, her bright eyes still entranced by the unfolding action of the proud Frog King and the courageous fairy princess.

No chance of art imitating life up here in the royal balcony! Robyn plucked her work pager off her waistband and made a *What can you do?* shrug of apology, scooped up her raincoat and skulked out of the auditorium like the coward she felt.

When she dared to turn around and peek through the red velvet curtains, it was as if she had never been there at all. Amira's arm had snaked around her father's neck as he held her close. Father and daughter. An unbreakable bond.

Robyn turned and all but ran down the stairs, gulping in lungful after lungful of London's cool night air when she pushed through the double doors out onto the street. She held her arm up to hail a taxi, then abruptly dropped it. She could walk to the hospital from here.

A brisk walk would take thirty, maybe forty minutes from the West End given the amount of energy she had to burn. She'd limit herself to an hour at the hospital. Just a chance to peek in on the little sleeping faces. The ones she wouldn't let herself get attached to except, of course, on a professional basis. Hopefully, little Penelope Craig wouldn't be there. Too much time in the cardiology unit for that wonderful little girl.

With each click of her boot heels she added a mental note to her ever-growing tick list.

Sort out her surgeries.
One or two days max in Da'har.
Arm's length.

That was where she'd keep Amira. No more cuddling during the scary bits of West End musicals.

And, of course, her gloweringly attractive father would have to be sure he knew his place. The man had more than a little Mr. Rochester running through him. An image of herself as Jane

Eyre flickered into her head and out again when she remembered Jane had to have all that awful tumbling about in the moors in the cold and wet. August in Da'har would be sunny and enriching—not that desert kingdoms had ever been on her radar.

Would she get to wear a gauzy and enigmatically mysterious ensemble? Curly toed silk shoes? Ride a camel?

Her foot caught on the pavement and she only just stopped herself from taking a nosedive onto the hard concrete.

Serves you right, daydreamer.

Back to the checklist.

Her mind shot into the familiar gear of Only Look Forward, Do Not Look Back as the rain began to fall around her in a mist. At first it added a bit of ambience to the evening until heaven wearied of its indecision and cranked open a full-blown downpour.

List-making became more succinct at this point.

Perform the surgery.
Don't get attached. To anyone.
Job done.

"A *fortnight*?"

Idris held the phone away from his ear and

looked at the receiver as if he were going mad. Most people would give their right arm to stay at the palace for a day let alone a couple of weeks. He cleared his throat, drew a swift outline of a bird on the hotel notepad and tried again.

"Yes, Dr. Kelly. A fortnight."

Silence.

He obliterated the bird under a thick layer of lead, snapping the pencil tip off in the process. He didn't know why, but this whole business of getting Robyn on board felt more akin to…wooing than asking and receiving.

"Dr. Kelly—a fortnight or we go elsewhere."

Robyn stared at her phone receiver—almost expecting to see Idris's face through some sort of telephonic portal. When she heard him continuing, the irritation in his tone made her relieved this wasn't a teleconference.

"Kaisha will sort out all the particulars and I will be the contact for everything involving Amira and her medical treatment."

"There's no need for that."

"Yes," he said. "There is."

"Whatsoever you desire, Your Excellency."

Since when had she morphed into a courtier?

Robyn hung up the phone without any of the usual niceties and stared out into the corridor where the hustle and bustle of Paddington's continued as if nothing at all had changed in the world.

It had, though. All of the fear that had been gripping the hospital as it rallied its troops under the threat of closure had just taken on a seismic shift. And the responsibility for which direction that shift took was on her. She could almost imagine a tiny halo-wearing Victoria appearing on her shoulder and asking, "Well, Robyn? Are you going to save us?"

She tried to picture Idris with a little pair of horns and a trident on the other shoulder, but he kept turning into a shirtless Poseidon standing—poised for action—at the prow of a beautiful handmade ship, willing to do anything for his daughter's well-being. Even acquiescing, just a little, to an ENT specialist if it meant his little girl would hear one day.

The sacrifices parents made for their children never failed to humble her. The very same sacrifices she would have given to have a child of her own.

Just thinking of Amira brought back the incredible sensation of holding her in her arms last night at the theater. The little-girl limbs, all curled up, sending out wafts of little-girl scent…

"Knock-knock?" Victoria rapped lightly on Robyn's door frame. Victoria wasn't wearing her usual paramedic uniform. She looked like she was power dressing for a meeting. Another reminder of just how important the decision she'd made to go to Da'har was.

Robyn stared at Victoria for a moment, realizing her arms were still holding the invisible child on her lap. She dropped her hands, limp and empty, to hang by her sides. The ache for a child to love would never be appeased.

"So? Are you packing your bikini and sunblock?"

"Ha! I don't think that's considered traditional garb in Da'har."

Victoria looked at Robyn closely. She was good at reading people and today was no different.

"You don't *have* to go, you know."

That answered that, then.

Victoria's brow crinkled with concern, her hand unconsciously slipping to her very pregnant tummy.

Robyn looked away and then up to Victoria's kind, hazel gaze.

"The problem is, my friend, not whether I can bear to go…but whether I can bear *not* to."

"With the future of the hospital at stake, you mean?" Victoria bravely put words to the elephant in the room.

"Yeah." Robyn nodded. "Which is why I said yes."

Victoria's face lit up, her face a real-life version

of the sunbeam smiley face on her notepad. "You did? Oh, that's great, Robyn. It's really great! I'm off to meet the board now so I'll let them know." She stepped away from the door frame, then quickly poked her head back into Robyn's office. "If that's all right."

"Of course it's all right." Robyn nodded, laughing at Victoria's burst of enthusiasm. "Now, leave me be. I've got tons to do before I can even think about sunblock!"

"Ugh…" Victoria sighed, leaning her cheek against the doorframe. "I'm totally jealous. The beautiful ocean, the warmth, the freshly squeezed orange juice and the amazing baguettes… And fruit! Think of the amazing fruit bowls—"

"Don't you have a meeting to go to?" Robyn stemmed the flow of excitement with a faux schoolmarm purse of the lips. One aimed more at herself than Victoria. She needed to see this as work only. Not pleasure. "You're making me hungry."

Victoria left with a flutter of her fingers, humming as she went.

At least she'd made *someone* happy.

With fresh resolve, Robyn pulled her keyboard across the notepad full of doodles, masking the grumpy face and thundercloud.

The next few weeks weren't going to be so

much of a trip into the unknown as a magic carpet ride into a world where anything was possible.

Fingers crossed that "anything" included restoring Amira's hearing. If the surgery failed?

She gave a quick thumbs-up to Ryan as he steamed by on his crutches.

The surgery couldn't fail.

The hospital's future depended upon it.

CHAPTER FOUR

IDRIS'S STRIDE WAS a single long-legged one to her two. Maybe even two and a half. Robyn was no shorty, but she was practically having to skip to keep up with him. And it wasn't as if she'd *asked* him to show her to her room, so he could drop the whole "being put upon by her presence" thing. Surely a sheikh would have at least a handful of servants to hand. And yet…there'd been no one other than Sheikh Idris Al Khalil himself opening the door to a very un-palace-like palace when the driver dropped her in the semicircular drive of the stone-and-clay building nestled amongst an acre or two of lush gardens.

She ran a few steps, making an exaggerated clatter on the tiles as she eventually caught up.

"It's really beautiful," she tried.

"I'm so pleased you think so."

His body language was the opposite of a delighted host. Didn't they do charm school in Da'har?

Then again, she had been very reluctant to agree to come in the first place so maybe they were a match made in heaven.

Ha! When cats could fly. Or something like that.

"I trust this will do?" Idris flung open a pair of intricately carved wooden doors and stepped to the side so that Robyn could enter the bedroom... or...was it an entire *suite* of rooms?

"Idris, it's—" She gave him a gob-smacked double take. "That was a rhetorical question, right?"

Her question went unanswered. Just a slight tightening of those sensual lips.

"It's beautiful, but I don't need—"

He raised his hand and shook his head. "We'd like you to be happy with your rooms during your stay here."

Robyn bit back a less than civil response that might have included words like *enforced* and *commanded* and instead reminded herself that the entire reason for being here in Da'har was because of Paddington's. And one very darling little girl.

"We can put you up in another suite if this isn't to your liking."

"No!" She waved him off as if "settling" for the grouping of rooms she could have easily fit her entire flat into was something she could just about come to terms with. It was the only cover she could come up with to mask the fact she was all but drooling over everything her eyes had lit upon so far.

Four stories of stone, jewel-colored tiles rose above a massive internal courtyard of the palace, whose centerpiece was a vast shallow pool tiled with what looked like millions of little squares and diamonds. A virtual jungle flourished and tumbled from the plenitude of balconies, dipping their jungle green leaves into the expansive pool.

Who knew such a place existed? Perhaps it was where they washed His Royal Excellency's rose petals.

She sniggered, then quickly covered her mouth, aware she was very likely suffering from a severe case of visual overload.

Idris impatiently cleared his throat, to which Robyn offered a polite smile in return. She took a few steps into the room, shoes immediately sinking into sumptuous carpets her high-heels-weary toes just itched to dig into. What had she been thinking when she'd put the ruddy things on in the first place?

Dressing to impress?

Hardly.

She twiddled her toe around a swirly design on the carpet, reminding herself she was here for work and to spend time with Amira.

"Out here is your courtyard." Idris had disappeared from her side and was opening a pair of French windows leading to a lushly gardened patio.

"If you like you can take your breakfast here—"

"Oh! I thought I'd be dining with Amira," Robyn cut in, flopping back onto the bed and only just escaping suffocation by a generosity of silk-covered throw pillows…and a bouncy mattress, too!

She looked up at Idris from her prone position, aware her eyes were perhaps a little too sparkly after the playful bed-tester moment.

His gaze was penetrating and decidedly cool. Chilly slivers of discomfort shot through her veins. She was just testing the bed, for heaven's sake! Give a jet-lagged woman a break!

She pushed herself up awkwardly amid the sea of luxurious bedding, her eyes leaving his to seek purchase on item after item of discreet comforts and immaculate design.

Truthfully? She was still a bit shell-shocked from handing over her surgical roster. She'd lectured and double lectured the team on the importance of attention to detail before being practically pushed out of the hospital and into a waiting taxi by Victoria.

Then there was the first-class flight to Da'har. A first. She had automatically turned right upon boarding the plane and was instantly turned around and steered left by flight attendants who all seemed to have been briefed that she was a guest of His Excellency's.

"The en-suite bathroom is just through here."

Her eyes followed the length of Idris's fingers, loitered just a moment, wondering what their touch upon her skin would elicit, then zoomed past them on to an arched doorway.

Carved marble. *Natch.* To go with the intricately tiled floors that had stretched out before them as they'd worked their way from one end of the surprisingly comfortable palace to the other.

She looked at Idris, a bit taken aback to find his black eyes continuing their indecipherable inquisition.

"You wouldn't mind grabbing me a couple of extra towels, would you?"

Idris's eyes widened as his eyebrows all but shot past his hairline. His very thick, very rake-your-fingers-through-me hairline.

"Ha, ha!" Robyn made a goofy face. "Kidding!"

So much for acting all mature and aloof when she got here. What she wouldn't give for a pair of scrubs and a surgical theater.

She swung her shoulders side to side, wondering why on earth Idris was just standing there staring at her until she couldn't bear it any longer and braved breaking the awkward silence.

"Any chance of seeing Amira? Maybe she can give me the full Monty tour of your pal—palatial home." Still a little weird to call his house a palace. Still a little weird to be in Da'har.

"By 'full Monty' you mean…?"

One of Idris's eyebrows remained aloft while the other dipped into a studiously displeased crinkle.

"Um…" An image of jolly blokes down at the pub doing stripteases morphed into strobe-lit flickers of Idris tugging off his loose-fitting linen shirt to reveal—

She dragged her eyes away from the expanse of chest and forced herself to meet his detached gaze. She shifted, stupidly nervous he'd poked his head into her mental cinema and not enjoyed what he saw. He'd seen other things, too. Hurt. Loss. Defensiveness.

An urge to have him see more, know more about her, began to override her nerves, and retreated just as quickly. She didn't trust herself to share the real Robyn with a man who seemed to value his privacy as much as she did.

"I'd love to see the place through Amira's eyes and I'm sure you're very busy with, um, ruling your kingdom?"

"I've largely cleared my schedule for the duration of your visit."

Ah.

Unexpected.

Unwanted.

"Not to tend to me, I hope!"

"More to look out for my daughter's interests," he replied dryly.

"Of course."

How could haughty and arrogant look so… so…*rip my clothes off, please*?

Actually, there probably wouldn't even be a "please" in there. Just commands and expectations of obedience.

Which opened a whole other doorway to sexy she'd never thought of before.

Robyn's cheeks streaked with heat. She was going to have to find something to blame for all of the illicit thoughts crowding out her common sense. She seemed to have left the Robyn whose life was only about Paddington's back in customs.

That Robyn was familiar. That Robyn she could deal with. *That* Robyn had something to fill her every waking moment with! Patients. Surgeries. Research.

This one? The one thinking all sorts of sassy inappropriate things while waiting to see a little girl who was tucked away somewhere in this cavernous palace? This Robyn was really, really in need of something to do.

Idris turned sidelong to her—offering next to no signs of leaving and absolutely no show of being satisfied with what he saw as his ebony eyes raked the length of her.

There might have been a few meters separating them, but his eyes didn't just look...they *inspected*. His gaze felt tactile.

Being naked in front of a million penguins would've felt less awkward.

Her nicest and most conservative "London suit" was making her feel itchy and trapped. When she'd landed, she'd been surrounded by men wearing weather-appropriate *dishdashas*—the collarless ankle-length gowns that looked more cooling than constraining. As did the women's *abayas*. Long, loose-fitting fabrics fluttering prettily in the breeze seemed far more appealing than her snug wool skirt and jacket combo. Blasted British summer! It had been perfect ten hours ago in London.

Idris was wearing Western clothing—a loose-fitting linen top and dark linen trousers—but unlike her, he seemed entirely unaffected by the late-afternoon heat.

Robyn rocked back on her stupidly uncomfortable "business" heels and gave her new...what was he? Boss? Benefactor? Whoever he was, she gave him a sidelong look that she hoped showed him the last thing she was going to do with her time—her precious time—was stand here like a von Trapp child waiting for the whistle blow that would allow her to be dismissed and *do something*. Idle hands and all that.

"Is there some sort of code word I'm meant to be using? Something that will get the ball rolling here?"

Idris's eyebrows tucked together in the center of his forehead and just as quickly drew apart. "You've never had a holiday, have you, Dr. Kelly?"

Who made you Mr. Insightful of the Year?

"Perhaps there's an element of truth to what you say…" she allowed, wondering why she was speaking like an eighteenth-century duchess.

"Have you not ever done anything just for fun, Dr. Kelly?"

Why did he keep saying her name all the time? He'd charmed her into agreeing to leave the hospital; it was fair to say they could follow through on the first-name basis thing.

"It's Robyn," she said through gritted teeth. "And I think we've got a little case of the pot calling the kettle black here, don't you?"

She suddenly realized, as the words hit their intended target, that the two of them were birds of a feather. Maybe not in the billionaire-ruler-of-a-country department, as she ran a department that could easily *spend* a billion…or two.

But in the all work and no play department,

Idris seemed as ill at ease with this unexpected "holiday" as she did.

She stood there, unexpectedly transfixed as Idris processed what she'd said. It was, it slowly dawned upon her, unlikely that people ever spoke to him so…frankly. Saw that his solid stance, indecipherable mood and cool response to her agitated shuffling were all defense shields against the less protected business of being human.

Their gazes meshed and the shock waves of heat detonating throughout her body at the union were unlike anything she'd experienced before.

She didn't dare think how she'd respond if they were actually touching.

A shudder of awareness shifted down her spine as she tried to regain control, knowing if she were to open her heart to the man standing before her, she would be powerless to defend herself.

Idris abruptly turned on his heel and left the room. *Her* room.

The one where Robyn would undress tonight and stretch, catlike no doubt, along the length of the bed that he wished he hadn't seen her enjoying so much.

What had he been thinking inviting Robyn to Da'har? To the palace? His *home*? The one place he could hide away from the world and all of the things he didn't want to feel.

Yes, he wanted Robyn to get to know Amira, his cherished little girl, but had he really wanted things to feel so personal?

His jaw tightened at the thought.

Absolutely not was the answer to that one.

He tried to hold back the surge of attraction he'd felt for Robyn just now in long-legged purposeful strides toward his office.

"Daddy!"

His daughter jumped out from behind a tree in the central courtyard, signing his name and mouthing the word in the Da'har dialect he longed for her to hear.

He scooped her up into his arms and swung her around, tightly embracing Amira in his arms as he wheeled around to find Robyn standing at the far end of the courtyard.

"Yes?" he asked, placing his daughter on the cobalt-and-jade-colored tiled bench surrounding the fountain.

"I—I was looking for Amira." Robyn faltered, eyes still locked on his until in a swish and a whirl, Amira, too, saw Robyn and flew from the fountain's edge up and into Robyn's arms as if she were a long-lost...

Oh, no. He didn't dare say "mother." But the smile that lit up on Robyn's face as she scooped his child up in her arms? It was loving. Unrestricted by the cruelty of life as his was.

A sting of jealousy went through him as he saw the pair of them, gabbling away in a mix of heaven knew what, fingers flashing, eyebrows jigging around, mouths exaggerating words.

Idris caught himself staring at Robyn's lips—a beautiful dusky shade of rose—and for the second time felt a rush of attraction he hadn't thought possible. Whether it felt like betrayal or destiny he couldn't tell. The first word that came to his head told him all he needed to know.

Malikah.

His wife's birth name had crowned her queen before he had fallen in love and made her a true one. Never had the nation known such collective joy as the day they had married.

Never had the nation borne such grief as the day she had died giving birth to their daughter.

This precious jewel of his who was— His eyes zapped across the courtyard. Was Amira laughing?

His eyes widened as he took in the sight and rarely heard sound of his daughter's laughter. Robyn was tickling Amira's little tummy, eliciting burble after burble of giggly laughter.

Extraordinary.

She was normally such a stern little girl.

Took after her father, everyone said. Took her future responsibilities incredibly seriously for such a young child.

He'd taken the words as praise. Had felt *prideful* his daughter's tendencies were to take seriously the role she would eventually hold as Sheikha, and yet…

The sound of her laughter—more beautiful than that of all the birdsong in the land—swept a slash of doubt across his clean conscience.

Robyn rose from her kneeling position and took Amira's hand in hers, realigning her features into a hopeful expression.

"Amira and I need your help," she said.

"Oh?"

Winning comeback, Your Excellency. And since when did he speak to himself in the third person? Life had made certain he knew that he, too, was only human when his wife had been taken from him. He shook his head. Robyn might be suffering from jet lag but he was suffering from…brain lag.

"Yes, we need your help." Robyn signed something to Amira, who turned her expression, now very grave, toward him. "We've got a bit of a language barrier and hoped you could help."

Amira mouthed and signed their "secret" language. They'd developed it over the years as a sort of father-daughter shorthand. And right now his daughter was very emphatically telling him Robyn's shoes were silly, too hot to be worn in

Da'har, and needed to be changed. As was her suit. They should go to the souk.

Idris's eyes widened.

She'd never asked such a thing before.

They rarely left the palace grounds excepting public celebrations where he and his security team could keep their watchful eyes upon her.

"We can get someone to fetch everything Robyn needs," Idris replied.

"It could be fun!" Robyn interjected. "I've never been to the souk," she added, her shy smile prizing apart his decision not to leave the grounds.

"Nor has Amira." Idris addressed this solely to Robyn in a tone few would mistake as approving. There was a reason this was so. Why her outings were predominantly only for state occasions.

The crowds, the frenetic bustle, the chaotic mayhem the market could burst into without a moment's notice. Even with bodyguards he had never thought the journey appropriate. Not for a little girl. Not *his* little girl.

"It would be madness if we were to just appear at the souk." He pressed his heels against the tiled floors, rising to his full height. "Not *fun*."

He felt a tug on his hand.

Amira's fingers wrapped around just one of his as her other hand curled into a soft little fist and rubbed in a circle over her heart.

Please.

Sign language was an evocative thing.

Her expression mirrored the word.

Please.

He thought back to his own childhood. Free of bodyguards. Endless hours wandering the souks and sprawling communities fanning out from the exquisitely designed city center. Speaking to the people whose lives he would one day hold responsibility for. Listening...

Exactly!

Listening.

It would be difficult for Amira. Too difficult. Too many people who would crowd and surround her, keen to tell her their stories with no means of communicating.

Stories she might one day hear if this infuriating blond woman standing in front of him, elbows akimbo, loosely curled hands propped on hips, would see some ruddy sense in the decisions he made.

No souk.

Not today.

He felt a tug on his fingers and looked down at the little, expectant face tipped up toward his.

Two against one.

He rolled his eyes heavenward only to have them land on a smiling Robyn upon their descent.

This, he was beginning to think, was going to be an awfully long fortnight.

"This is such fun, don't you think?" Robyn smiled cheerfully, seemingly immune to Idris's increasingly dark mood as they obeyed his daughter's insistent beckoning to enter another clothing store.

Idris made a noncommittal grunt. *Fun* wasn't exactly the word he would've chosen. The perfect recipe for an ulcer was more like it. Ditching the security guards at his daughter's insistence meant he was the one weighted with the bags and boxes of clothing and scarves Robyn had accrued.

Thus far.

Or should he say, the items Amira had accrued on Robyn's behalf. The poor woman was as powerless as he was in the face of Amira's untapped shopping gene.

Idris ruled, with meticulous detail, an entire *kingdom*, for goodness' sake! And here he was being pulled willy-nilly down the never-ending twists and turns of the maze that was the capital city's largest souk.

"Just one more?" His daughter struck her most forlorn and wide-eyed expression.

He had to smile as she didn't bother waiting for an answer and tugged him into the store—walls all but hidden by silks, tunics and headscarves.

Robyn's arrival seemed to have transfigured

his serious little girl into little less than a high-powered personal shopper as she inspected the beautiful fabrics and clothing items on display, then casting an appraising eye over Robyn, who was, he had to admit, playing along rather wonderfully.

She would turn and sashay and kneel down so Amira could hold the fabrics up to her strawberries-and-cream complexion, every now and again, flicking those amber eyes up to meet his for what exactly he wasn't sure.

Approval?

The stirrings of something he hadn't felt in a long time—seven years to be precise—told him all he needed to know. They'd done enough shopping for today.

"I think your daughter would do well in Paris!" Robyn stood up, laughing, when Amira rejected another ream of richly colored *sarwals*—the formfitting trousers that drew a man's attention directly to a woman's ankle.

He could feel his jaw tighten at the thought of Amira growing up at all. His little girl. His precious little girl.

"My daughter does perfectly well in Da'har."

"I wasn't suggesting—" Robyn protested, then stopped, her eyes glued to his as if trying to divine why he'd gone all prickly. "Of course she does," she said gently. "Just look at her."

His eyes stayed on Robyn just a moment longer as she turned to watch Amira inspecting pairs of traditional leather shoes much to the shopkeeper's delight. She used her own form of communicating, a mix of mouthing the words in the local Da'harian dialect and miming movements or pointing. She was never inhibited by her inability to communicate in the traditional fashion. Never one to behave as though she had a disability. For her, this was normal. A normal Idris couldn't bear for her to endure. She deserved every gift of the senses he had and more! She was his daughter, for heaven's sake! The woman standing next to him was the one who could make it possible. He hadn't realized how frightening it would be to invest so much faith in one person. So much hope.

For her part, Robyn appeared openly charmed with Amira's mad-dash shopping bonanza, her eyes shining with unchecked delight. What she didn't know was that the little girl, beaming, expertly folding and unfolding the headscarves, was *bargaining*, for heaven's sake, negotiating for this *dishdasha* or that pair of harem trousers— she wasn't the little girl he saw very often. And watching her come to life as she did with Robyn was more painful than he could have imagined.

They were moments Amira should be having with her mother. The mother she would never know. He turned again as Robyn joined his daughter, each of them running an appraising finger along the intricately designed sandals, their heads bent together—one black as midnight, the other impossibly golden—and his heart cinched even tighter.

"All right, then." His voice sounded jagged amid the happy buzz and hum that had filled the shop mere seconds earlier. "Time to go."

Drawing any sort of banter out of Idris on the car ride home was proving next to impossible. The pulling-blood-from-a-stone variety.

His jet-black eyes were trained on the roads as they whizzed past the beautiful structures that made up the old town. A vividly modern section of the city lay closer to the airport, looking every bit the hotbed of Middle Eastern business Da'har was purported to be.

She turned to peek at Amira, who had fallen asleep amid the tumble of boxes and shopping bags, her beautiful little face framed in tissue paper and silk ribbons.

Focusing very stoically on the beautiful capital city was the only way Robyn could stem a sudden stingy tickle and tease of tears. She scratched her nails along her legs as they balled into fists.

You can love her from a distance.

She squeezed her eyes tight.

You shouldn't let yourself love her at all.

"Everything all right?"

"Yes, fine." She looked up, surprised Idris had noticed her change of mood at all. "Just a long day, is all." *An endless future without a child of my own…*

"If you look just over to your right—" he slowed the speed of the four-by-four "—you will see the Museum of Swords."

"Of *swords*?"

"Absolutely. There are a few of my father's in there and—" he chuckled more to himself than her as if remembering the rake of a man he may once have been "—one or two of mine."

Clear as day she saw Idris tugging not one but two wide-lipped scimitars from horn-and-ivory cases, crossing the flashing blades in front of him, shielding Robyn and Amira from…camel-riding marauders intent on kidnapping them from their Bedouin tent—carpets and all!

"Goodness."

Idris unleashed a full-throated laugh at her prim, English response. Little did he know she was busy A-Thousand-and-One-Nighting it now that she had a more appropriate wardrobe. Or was it the *someone* playing the dashing knight who'd unbuckled her imagination?

She felt her lips purse at the thought, barely hearing him as he talked her through each of the buildings they passed.

She didn't *fancy* Idris.

He was too…too gorgeously unattainable to plain old crush on.

Unh-unh. Apart from which, there was the very obvious point that men like him didn't desire people like her. He was serious to her scatty. He could do limelight. She'd rather hide in an operating theater than be the object of attention. He was a sun, she was an orbiting moon—happy to enjoy the light and heat and *electricity* of his presence from afar.

Hmm. Maybe she did fancy him. Just a little.

Her gaze lowered and slid toward him as she tilted her chin to make it look like she was memorizing the facts he was rattling off rather than ogling him.

Idris Al Khalil was beautifully sensuous in the most masculine of ways. Strong-featured. Stoic. Commanding. And she? While they were about the same age, she felt past any sort of prime she might have had. No, she wasn't *old*, but…losing the ability to have children all that time ago seemed to have stolen something from her. Perhaps as losing his wife had stolen that rare, wonderful laugh from Idris. Her fingers pressed into her lips to stem a sigh.

"And this, over here—" she followed his fingers as they lifted off the steering wheel and pointed to her left "—is the Old Castle."

The structure rose from the ground as if it had been there a thousand years. More opulent fortress than French château, there were acres of towers and soaring walls, wooden shuttered windows closed against the late-afternoon sun that made the air smell hot and heavily spiced.

"So, you live in the…New Castle?"

Again, Idris laughed, but as it faded away, so, too, did the light she'd seen in his eyes as he pointed out the architectural jewels in his family's crown.

"No," he replied. Then again, harder. Flintier. "No."

He turned a corner from one street to the next, the light shifting to a rosy golden hue as the sunset caught the harbor city in its full glory.

"This was the New Castle."

A broad avenue stretched out before them. Something akin to the Mall leading up to Buckingham Palace. Something fit for a king. At the top of the avenue was a gloriously modern structure, resplendent in its nod to traditional architecture, unerring in its thrust toward the future.

It was a modern-day Taj Mahal, she knew at once. No longer a palace to be lived in, but a seven-year-old testament to love.

Out of the corner of her eye, she saw Amira stir and wake, her eyes blinking into understanding as to where she was. Her little hands pressing against the window as she blew kisses to her mother's tomb.

Another hit of emotion burned the rims of Robyn's eyes so strongly she was forced to turn away from it all. Idris's stoic profile, the little girl lost in thought over a mother she'd never know and a palace standing in the midst of Da'har's many people—empty and alone.

CHAPTER FIVE

"LET'S HAVE A fashion show, shall we?"

Robyn looked as astonished as Idris felt hearing that collection of words coming out of his mouth.

Fashion show?

And yet...

All of their moods had taken a discernible dip after they returned but somehow the somber atmosphere didn't seem fitting with Robyn around.

He'd had seven years of walking around like the god of thunder and retribution, perhaps a new turn as...something else was in order.

"Come along." He nodded toward the large pile of untouched boxes and paper-wrapped packages. "We weren't dragged across Sanhella's largest souk just to sit here watching you grow more and more uncomfortable in that suit of yours."

A hot flash of primal instinct took hold of him as he pictured Robyn revealing for them, veil by veil, the layers of delicate silks and diaphanous wraps concealing her slender figure, currently unartfully hidden in the boxy suit she'd arrived in.

"I really don't think that's necessary." Robyn shook her head, clearly uninterested in displaying her wares, silken or otherwise.

A flush crept up the length of her neck as she busied herself with finishing off a savory pastry parcel they'd brought home from the souk, a parting gift from a vendor who'd spotted them loading up Robyn's purchases.

"I insist," he said, wincing at the unintended harshness in his tone, and tacked on smile, hoping it would soften the moment. He'd have to work on his "order" voice before Amira could hear. He'd have to work on a lot of things.

He glanced over at his daughter innocently finishing the picnic dinner they'd opted to have in the central atrium, her little brows furrowed together in their usual cinch as she worked out the spices and scents each savory morsel afforded.

There were servants and formal dining rooms and even more formal rooms for impressing visitors in the government buildings—not too far away—but this house he'd designed after Amira was born was their sanctuary.

He was surprised to realize having Robyn in his home felt right. As if she were someone who immediately saw it for what it was—a retreat from the world and a reminder of everything that was beautiful as his heart fought the darkness that so often threatened to consume him.

"Would a single showing along the catwalk suffice?" Robyn asked as a put-upon soldier might inquire of a general demanding his boots be polished every fifteen minutes.

He nodded curtly. Too curtly given the internal ticking off he was giving himself for just that sort of brusque behavior. Behavior that had near enough held everyone he had once loved at arm's length. Friends, advisers—aunts and uncles who no longer knew how to deal with the coldness he knew exuded from him the day his heart had all but withered and died. The only thing that had kept him alive was the little girl sitting across from him. The one throwing him a "fix it now, Daddy" look as Robyn's discomfort increased.

"Please," Idris asked, palms turned upward in an open appeal to her generous spirit. "Please show us how you look in your new outfits."

Under Idris's dark-eyed gaze…Robyn felt as if there was no escape. As if he were looking straight through to her very soul. His long-lashed eyes easily swept aside the bluster and Englishness she hid behind, seeing instead the particles making up the invisible essence that was her spirit. The very kernel of who she'd become in the aftermath of her painful loss. And yet he didn't know a thing.

That she was a woman who ached. A woman

who felt the loss of her unborn child as if it had happened yesterday.

Idris moved his hands forward in a genuine entreaty for her indulgence, eyes shifting toward Amira, then back to hers.

The request wasn't just for him. It was for his daughter, and no points for guessing how powerless she was in that department.

Little Amira had all but wrapped her around her finger and she'd only been in the country a handful of hours. Ridiculous!

She swept some invisible crumbs off her cheeks, hoping the gesture made excuses for the pink she knew was there, and pushed up from the cluster of pillows she'd been leaning on while they ate.

"There's a powder room off to the left," Idris directed once she'd filled her arms with packages, much to Amira's delight.

Of course there was.

And, if she asked, there would probably be someone to come along and help her figure out how to make the best of the meters and meters of fabric Amira had selected. The fact there wasn't a collection of servants lining the atrium had her feeling grateful, if not a little surprised, that Idris seemed to live so privately.

The palace bore a far more personal touch than she would have suspected. Idris was all cut glass and black marble, but this place—this *home*—looked as if someone had conjured up the mythical Hanging Gardens of Babylon. But, as he'd told her over supper, it had all come from Idris—from his thesis project in university where he'd studied architecture and, of course, politics.

What a project! A love letter to the traditional architecture of his land, with secret, little hidden-away connections to the modern world. Wi-Fi, built in radios, tablets lying out of sight, but always within reach, if ever a person wondered what if...and the answer was only a tip and a tap of a keyboard away.

The more he spoke, the more she saw this place was the dream child of his complicated mind, the heart that had known such sorrow and a mind that bore, surprisingly, an extraordinary imagination. For a man who came across as being utterly rigid about his beliefs and ways, his home was almost whimsical.

She turned just before going into the changing room and saw he was watching her. Two of the boxes tumbled out of her hands and as she lurched to catch them she managed to lose her grip on the bags dangling precariously from her fingertips.

She dropped almost gratefully to the floor to collect everything up, then crawled into the changing room—mercifully out of sight.

Wow, did she hate the limelight.

* * *

"Another one!"

Robyn gave a playful eye roll and turned back toward the changing room.

So far they'd seen three outfits and, with each one, Robyn had softened and relaxed in the "glare" of her audience's eyes.

Idris felt a tug on his sleeve. His daughter was facing him, her face alight with excitement and hands whirling with a rapid-fire list of demands.

Pull the curtains together. Robyn needed a place to have a "proper" entrance. Where was her dress-up box? Could she please wrap his head in a turban and draw on a mustache. Why should Robyn be the only one to dress up?

Laughing, he pulled his daughter into his arms, rose and swirled her around, eliciting squeals of delight as he swung her over the fountain's edge.

A phone call later, boxes appeared and Idris found himself near enough nose-to-nose with his daughter.

Robyn peeked out from the changing rooms only to find curtains had been drawn between the two columns she had been using as a stage. She'd heard Amira's squeals earlier, and now could hear the little girl's laughter. She chanced a glance between the curtains, her own lips twitching into a smile as she saw the scene unfolding before her.

With a face as serious as a general's, Amira had one hand planted on her father's head as she fastidiously went about drawing on the curliest mustache Robyn had ever seen with the other. Idris sat patiently, his caramel skin becoming less visible beneath the swirling magnificence of his daughter's artwork. Amira pulled back and eyed her handiwork. Idris pulled a couple of faces, giving the drawn-on mustache life and eliciting another peal of laughter from his daughter. Next, she pulled a length of opalescent silk out of a wooden crate and gave it swirl after swirl upon his head until he had a beautifully wrapped turban atop his head. He jumped up and struck a pose on the side of the fountain for her, feigned losing his balance so well Robyn almost jumped through the curtains to help—

Help what? Interrupt a beautiful moment between a father and daughter? For every part of her that ached to be with them, enjoying the moment, there was another part reminding her that this was not her world. Not her life. Arriving in Da'har had felt akin to handing over her passport to a different universe. Not just the different sights and sounds, but different feelings, responses. She sucked in a deep breath. English Robyn would run back to her room and hide rather than show off the outfit she felt strangely at home in. She blew the breath out, pulled her shoulders back and

smiled. She wasn't English Robyn right now—
she was the Little Bird of Da'har and she felt as
though she could fly.

"How's this?" Robyn asked, sweeping open the
drapes of the changing rooms and spinning along
the "catwalk" in a swirl of diaphanous fabrics.
The light chiffon lifted and floated as Robyn's
hips and shoulders shifted and moved against the
silky softness.

Idris looked up and was instantly mesmerized.
If Robyn was amused by his mustache and tur-
baned look, she didn't show it. If anything, she
looked emboldened.

As she sauntered one moment, then twirled another, Robyn looked as he imagined she would
have as a younger woman—a giggling girl playing dress-up. And at times, when his eyes caught
with hers, he saw a woman discovering a sensuality blossom within her. A sensuality she'd never
known she possessed.

Until now.

Idris sat upright, utterly transfixed as their
eyes locked. His body grew taut with desire for
her.

He wanted Robyn. Wanted to pull her to him,
shift away the deep emerald chiffon and lace
headscarf with a sweep of his fingertips. His
hand twitched. One step led to the next as imag-

ination and desire melded into one. He would take hold of the back of her head, his other hand slipping onto the weightless silk that caressed her back and pulled her to him so that he could taste the bright red of her lips, her mouth. Urgently. Hungrily.

The sound of his daughter's clapping jarred him into the present. Into reality.

Their eyes still caught together, Robyn's body frozen mid-twirl, Idris tried to communicate all the things he couldn't say—couldn't put a voice to. As Robyn's eyes widened, then narrowed with understanding, shame and anger obliterated the romantic notions.

Robyn wasn't here to be his lover. Not even a friend. Her presence here was strictly business and he was a fool to think—even for a moment—she could be anything to him but a means to an end. The solution to his daughter's plight.

"Perhaps we've had enough fun for tonight."

"Yes," Robyn said. "I think I'll turn in straightaway if you don't mind." She turned to go, tripping as she did. The first time that night. For the past hour she'd felt beautiful. Graceful.

Amira rushed up to her when she realized Robyn was leaving and wrapped her arms around her waist.

Robyn gave her a quick squeeze and dropped

a kiss on top of her head, then hightailed it to her room, desperate to hide the tears she knew would come.

"Excellent!" Robyn accepted the pile of folders from Dr. Hazari. "These are all of her records?"

"His Excellency said to ensure you had everything you need."

Robyn didn't need a mirror to tell her that her eyebrows were knitting together. All she wanted was a little "me time" at a hospital. Amira's actual records were just a bonus.

"Has he—? You haven't spoken with him this morning, have you?"

"Of course," he said. "Her Royal Excellency's medical papers aren't something we just hand over to anyone."

"No," she said. "Of course not." She looked at the papers and then back to Dr. Hazari. "And you just pick up the phone and call him?"

"On matters relating to Amira—yes. Absolutely. He is always available to speak when it is about his daughter."

"How very...*accessible* of him." No staff, no go-betweens. A protective lion of a father.

She gave Dr. Hazari a smile of thanks, turned her attentions to the files and found she could only see one thing.

Idris Al Khalil.

The caramel skin. The proud set of his cheekbones drawing her attention first to the ebony sheen of his eyes, then tugging her along the descent toward the full, deep red of his mouth. Her pulse quickened at the memory of his lips parting when she had last appeared "onstage," an emerald headdress skating along the edges of her blond hairline, an even deeper green *dishdasha* skimming her skin as Idris's inky gaze unleashed prickles of anticipation across her entire body.

The man had haunted her dreams. That alone had been miracle enough because sleep had been a long time coming after she'd left him and those hauntingly evocative eyes of his.

Enough!

She snapped the folders into a precise pile and began meticulously working her way through them, ignoring the little tugs and pulls of guilt teasing away the well-stitched hemline of her conscience. So what if she'd snuck out of the palace and found her way to the hospital on her own. That's what guidebooks were for. Right?

A few hours in the hospital wouldn't hurt anyone. Especially not the impenetrable fortress that was Idris.

She squeezed her eyes shut against the image that had kept her awake well into the night. Idris's usually implacable expression softened.

A smile crept onto her lips. And it wasn't just

the memory of his swirly mustache. It was the whole picture. The proud father indulging an excited daughter. The host enjoying his guest's discovery of his country, his home. It was a side to Idris she suspected few people saw. A warm, loving family man at home with face painting and a spontaneous fashion show.

And when their eyes had met?

She couldn't help a little happy hum as she relived the moment. Idris's gaze had held something stronger in them than approval. They had sparked and fought the same thing she was feeling when she looked at him. Desire.

She sucked in a deep breath and held it.

Longing. Passion. Love.

She didn't do those sorts of things. Not now. Definitely not in the future. And all because of the past she'd never laid to rest. A past she'd had to deal with on her own.

How quickly news of an unexpected pregnancy had turned into the darkest of horror films. She'd been so happy. A wonderful boyfriend. Maybe a marriage? The ectopic pregnancy. Too advanced. Low to no survival rate. For herself and the child unless…

She looked up from the sofa where she'd been sitting and wondered if her subconscious had led her here.

The maternity ward.

Just like any hospital she'd ever been to, there was the row of beautiful babies, swaddled in soft blankets of pink or blue. Little eyes clenched tight against the world they'd only just entered, lips puckering, fingers reaching for the mother they were inextricably linked to.

Her baby hadn't come to term before they'd had to end the ectopic pregnancy threatening her life...but, oh, how she had ached to hold him. *Would* ache so long as she drew breath. It still astonished her how impossible it was to forget that tiny little child.

The breath released from her chest in a whoosh of regret.

She picked up her phone and did a quick calculation. Too early to call the hospital. Then again, surely *someone* she knew would be on night shift. She tapped the little green phone receiver icon, needing to hear a familiar voice.

"Is this how you always conduct your research?"

A shiver of recognition slipped along her spine, pooling in her belly.

Maybe not that particular voice.

She looked up from the phone, scanned past the pair of long legs, along the arms crossed over a linen-shirted chest and up, past the...stubble? Interesting. Idris was normally immaculately well-shaven.

"If you mean by going to a hospital to look at all of Amira's records, then yes," she replied with more verve than she felt.

She stood so she felt less like a five-year-old being told off outside the headmistress's office. It didn't stop her cheeks from burning, though. As she rose, Idris didn't take the customary step back one generally hoped for in the personal space department. Proximity only made her response to him deepen. She tilted her chin up and met his gaze with as much defiance as she could muster. Difficult, when her body was a bit busy doing its own thing—heart rate accelerating, the whoosh and roar of her body temperature soaring as her eyes met his. The physical need to reach out and touch him was near enough overwhelming every practical bone in her body.

"I meant sneaking out of the house and causing great distress to my daughter, who thought you'd left. Thought you weren't interested enough in spending time with her to do the surgery." His lips pressed together tightly as if he could've said more but was biting the words back against his better judgment.

All the swirly feelings swooping around Robyn's body like giddy hummingbirds plummeted into a weighted mass in her gut.

"I didn't think—"

"Precisely," Idris cut in. "You didn't think. I'm

hardly surprised to learn you don't have children of your own if this is how you treat children under your care."

From the streak of pain searing across Robyn's amber eyes, he knew in an instant he'd been cruel.

She stood, frozen in place, visibly digesting the sour spill of words he'd spat in anger. What could he have said instead? That he'd woken to discover an empty room, no sign of Robyn anywhere in the palace, his little girl's stricken face when she thought Robyn had fled? How could he tell her he'd been frightened, too? That he'd been left on his own again. That fear had manifested itself as rage.

"You'll be happy to hear, Your Excellency, I can't have children. A—a *procedure* I had in my twenties made sure of that."

He tore his gaze away from Robyn's, unable to bear the burden of guilt he bore for the sorrow in her eyes.

"I'm truly sorry," Robyn continued, her voice devoid of the light it usually carried. "I never meant to hurt Amira. Or to pull you away from her to hunt me down." Robyn gave the files a distracted look and swiped at her eyes where she'd lost the battle with a handful of tears. She looked up at him, cheeks flushed, voice hoarse with emotion. "And I never meant to hurt you."

In that moment, Idris was consumed by a need

to hold her in his arms until all the hurt and pain he'd caused went away. How could she be so generous with her apologies, so *heartfelt*, when he had been so unkind?

He opened his arms and pulled her toward him, unsurprised to feel her stiffen, then—much to his amazement—feel her relax into his embrace, laying her cheek against his chest as if seeking solace in the beat of his heart.

He did his best to steady his breath, quell the racket thumping around his rib cage, a little too aware of Robyn's wildflower scent, the soft femininity of her hand pressing against his chest.

He laid his cheek alongside her temple, astonished that Robyn, despite having seen his darker side, was bringing the man he'd once been back out into the light. The one who comforted, smiled and laughed. The one who enjoyed being *alive*!

For seven years he'd been shut off to that man. More attuned to one who saw the world through a filter of grief, frustration and fear for his daughter's well-being.

And yet, here he was, holding Robyn in his arms, conscience pricking at the harsh judgments he'd made as if he alone were bearing the weight of the world.

He traced his fingers along Robyn's temple, drawing them to her chin, only realizing as he caressed her cheek with the back of his hand that she was wearing a headscarf. Sky blue. It matched her personality, full of light and optimism.

The Da'harian style had seemed so natural on her when he'd first caught sight of her on the sofa; he hadn't even thought to remark on it. Or perhaps his relief at finding her had made him blind to everything else.

He held her close, neither of them saying anything, their breaths joining in a growing cadence with the other's.

They shared the understanding of loss. He knew that now.

This and a thousand questions filled his mind as he stroked her cheek with the backs of his fingers, relieved, at last, to feel her steadied breath upon his wrist. He crooked his index finger and tipped her chin up toward him, telling himself it was to ensure there were no more tears in her eyes, but the ease with which he could have leaned down and kissed her all but blindsided him.

Robyn blinked at his wide-eyed response to her, then gave a shy smile as she gently extricated herself from his embrace.

"Was that our first fight?"

"I suspect, my dear, it won't be our last."

My dear?

He checked himself. Best not to get too carried away. Emotions could far too easily take the helm when it came to Amira. They'd had a moment. Nothing more. He shook his head again, taking a step backward, only to barely avoid colliding with a passing nurse.

"Your Excellency!" The woman turned when she saw who he was, blanched and performed a quick bob.

He clucked away the gesture with a smile and a shake of the head. Adulation of any sort had never suited him. Earning the respect of his people was all that mattered.

"So!" He turned back to Robyn, masking his discomposure with what he hoped was a businesslike nod. "I suppose meeting our Ear, Nose and Throat specialists was on your tick list."

"Yes." She nodded, relieved to be back on familiar terrain. "I really would like to meet the entire team if possible. It would be particularly helpful to see where and who will be giving Amira her aftercare."

"Won't you be doing that?"

"Immediately after the surgery, of course I will, but…when you both return home, I'll be at Paddington's. Or wherever we end up if this closure goes ahead."

Her smile seemed unnaturally bright. As if she were forcing on the same show of bravura he was in the wake of the moment they'd just shared.

Pain, loss and the unexpected understanding that neither of them was alone.

The reminder that Robyn would be in and out of their lives so briefly shook the new sense of grounding he'd felt since she had come into their lives. He had borne so much alone that having her here felt like putting back together the pieces of a puzzle he'd never known had come apart.

"Well." He returned the artificially cheery smile. "Isn't it lovely we still have the best part of a fortnight together to sort out all the particulars? Now that I can allay Amira's fears about your mysterious vanishing, I trust I can safely leave you to your own devices here at the hospital for a handful of hours. We will, however, look forward to you joining us for lunch back home. And," he continued, trying his best not to stare as her mouth formed an inquisitive moue, "I hope you don't mind, but I have organized for some of your new things to be packed. We're going on a little trip this afternoon."

"Oh?"

His announcement seemed to have reduced her to monosyllables and widened eyes, but he noted with a satisfied smile that it was the first time she hadn't protested.

"Right, then." He gave a curt nod. "Shall I leave you in Dr. Hazari's capable care?"

Robyn nodded, her dazed expression mirroring everything he was feeling internally. There was something they shared now. A silent understanding of the burdens of grief. One he made no effort to hide from the world, while she… Robyn bore her grief for her own loss with tenacity and a fierce show of happiness. The light to his shade. The two essential components to make an object real.

He ground his teeth together and lengthened his stride. A walk rather than the high-speed drive he'd made to track Robyn down might be in order.

He was letting her under his skin. Too much. Too deep. And far too personal for his liking.

Robyn's presence here was solely for Amira, he reminded himself, putting meter after meter behind him in quick succession. None of this was personal excepting where it affected his daughter and her well-being. It was the only logical explanation for the surge of emotion he had experienced this morning.

He pushed open the doors to the hospital and looked out onto the busy street.

The early-morning bustle of the day sped past him as people went about their daily lives, blissfully unaware their leader was very busily trying to yank Cupid's wayward arrows out of his chest.

CHAPTER SIX

"WELL, THIS IS all a bit mysterious." Robyn tried her best to keep the trepidation out of her voice, but could see she'd been unsuccessful when Idris all but rolled his eyes.

So much for finding her way back into his good books. He'd been aloof ever since he'd left the hospital. Well. If aloof meant not around, then he had been extra aloof.

Not that she could blame him.

This was a business trip, not a touchy-feely sobfest about her bad luck in the procreation department. Her focus was meant to be on Amira and Paddington's future. Two diligent hours of work at the hospital later, she was back at the palace, wearing her best winning smile, trying to make up for the morning's unintended gaffe.

She felt a tug on her hand. Amira. "Do you like horses?" she asked.

"Very much." Robyn nodded emphatically. Riding had actually been one of her favorite escapes a few months after she'd had the hysterectomy. Work had been her first escape. But on the days she found being with the children at the hospital was too much to bear, she'd take herself away for the weekend, hire a horse at a stables and ride and ride and ride until the pain—for a moment at least—had ebbed away.

She looked up at Idris—something she seemed to do automatically now. Whether it was to check for his approval or to see what he was thinking she wasn't sure; all she knew was that in the space of a few days her mind's orbit had changed and Idris... She shook the thought away, reminding herself those who wore wax wings were never wise to fly too close to the sun.

"Are we going riding?"

"Something like that," Idris said with a quick nod.

No smile. No flash of a shared passion. Nothing. Subconscious or not, it told her one thing. She was here to learn and listen, not to get excited or become attached as too often happened when it came to the children who unwittingly pulled her heartstrings. With the way Amira was affecting her, Robyn was beginning to feel like the entire string section of a full-blown orchestra! No matter how hard she tried, remaining scientific and critically indifferent was impossible.

Caring made her a better doctor. But it came with a risk. Caring made the failures, or, more pointedly, the losses...cut too deep. That she was her own worst enemy was one way of looking at things. Hell-bent on destroying what little peace of mind she had would be more accurate.

Robyn squared herself to Idris wishing he'd treat her more like the highly respected surgeon she was than some thorn in his side. Being here, after all, wasn't her bright idea.

"Any chance you're going to tell me what it is we will be doing?"

A flash of irritation lit up his eyes. No attempt to try to hide it, either.

His behavior rankled. She felt as though Idris had thrown her into an emotional boxing ring. Round one, attacking her with his words, laying bare her biggest sorrow. Round two, pulling her into his arms, caressing her, holding her until her tears had dried. Now here she was in round three at arm's length again with little chance at gaining ground.

"We're going on a little trip. Away from the capital."

Amira nodded, her little heart-shaped face so earnest as she read her father's lips all the while weaving her fingers through Robyn's.

When their hands were as one, Robyn's heart skipped a beat—a warning sign that she was getting too close. Wanting too much to have a family of her own.

Idris reached across and took Amira's other

hand, compelling the little girl to release her own, take a hop-skip and stand by her father's side.

Knockout.

"I thought you might like to see some other parts of the country," Idris began, mercifully oblivious to her internal monologue. "It will be informative for you both to meet the people Amira will one day rule. See why her future, and the success of her operation, are so important."

Robyn looked down at the little girl, relieved to see a smile of anticipation on her face.

"Are we going to your favorite places?" Robyn signed and spoke.

Amira shook her head no, and gave a little jump of excitement.

"She's not traveled extensively in the country," Idris said, drawing Robyn's attention away from his daughter.

"Why not?"

It was a simple enough question but Idris seemed to need time to formulate the best answer. An overprotective parent? It was hard to blame him. She'd be gun-shy, too, in his shoes.

People began appearing out of doorways, arms full of luggage and packages.

"What's all this?"

"Supplies, mostly. Not all of it will be in the vehicle we take, but there will be a few follow-up trucks with us. I never like to go into the…less fortunate parts of Da'har without bearing gifts."

"I thought gift giving was normally *to* someone in your position, not the other way around," Robyn quipped lightly.

"No." Idris's lips tightened, his gaze darkening even further. "That's not the case in Da'har."

With a quick move of his eyes, she watched as he reminded himself his daughter was present. The man who ruled the land, the one setting an example for his daughter, took over the impatient, irritable one she seemed so easily to elicit.

"My family, just the two of us now—" he nodded to his daughter "—have benefited enormously from the natural resources of this kingdom. I make no show of hiding either my gratitude or my good fortune in being born into the ruling family of Da'har. It is inevitable that society—no matter the largesse of its leader—will suffer at least some inequalities."

Robin flushed under the intensity of his gaze as he spoke.

"There will always be people richer than others. Just as there will always be those who seem happier, more intelligent or naturally gifted with incomparable beauty."

He paused for a moment, eyes narrowing as they raked the length of her. If he was trying to tell her she was beautiful, he was going to have to work on the delivery. If he was trying to tell her otherwise... Her breath caught in her throat.

Don't go there, Robyn.

"We try to make the imbalance of life's offerings less obvious. Bringing gifts is our way of doing this. I thought we would also stop by the hospital. The storerooms will be made available to you if you'd like to collect some things and hold a small clinic for one or two of the tribal communities we will be visiting."

"Oh, I'd love that!" Robyn clasped her hands together, trying her best to push the "examination" out of her mind.

She bit down on her lower lip and watched as he delivered a few instructions to an approaching staff member. A part of her ached for him, was forgiving of his mood swings. He was a man doing his very best to find his place in the world after only just surviving the initial, suffocating waves of grief he must've experienced when he lost his wife. A man trying as best he could to raise his daughter.

A flurry of commotion took over as Amira's nanny appeared and took her away to change. Robyn's newly purchased clothes had disappeared from her room and were being loaded into a car somewhere inside the vast compound.

"Ten minutes. The car will be at the front of

the house. Don't be late," Idris instructed as he turned away to leave.

She nodded her assent, not that he was looking at her to notice, then looked around the extraordinary central courtyard of the house with fresh eyes. The fountains, the beautiful tiles, the comfort of it all…was this who Idris really was? Had inviting her here been his way of showing Robyn his gentler side?

She sat on the edge of the fountain, drawing her fingers across the surface of the pool, flowered lily pads moving in the tiny current she'd created. She wondered, for a moment, if this was what she'd done to Idris's life. Created a disturbance. Or—her lips turned up into a grin as she whirled her finger around in a circle—stirred things up for the better.

She looked up from the aqua pool, eyes moving from balcony to balustrade soaking in the beauty, trying to remind herself what she knew about Da'har.

Unlike similar kingdoms comprised of several tribes, Da'har had never experienced civil unrest. The rule—while held by one family—was far more progressive than in many of its neighboring countries. The city, what little she'd seen of it, sang of a place where tradition and progress met on an even footing. The same things were embodied, here in Idris's home. History and a look toward the future. A place that exemplified all that was good that had come from Da'har's rich, cultural past.

Such a contrast to the starkly modern palace he had been living in when he had been married. Perhaps, when there had been life and love in it, its sharp angles and cool facade had taken on a different hue.

She ran her fingers through the water again.

Idris's heart was in the past. It seemed to be the place where his decision making came from. That painful, hollowed-out place where light was a scourge to the grief he'd so clearly settled into.

How, she wondered, would his daughter be able to duck out from under his protective wing with an eye to the future?

A sigh whooshed out of her chest. The pair of them had so much responsibility. And, weighted with grief as Idris's story forever would be, could make seeing a new future—a *different* future—next to impossible.

"I feel like a chauffeur with the pair of you sitting back there!"

"We're very busy drawing everything we see," Robyn playfully retorted. "And hadn't you better keep your eyes on the road? Precious cargo and all that!" She was feeling strangely protective of the bond she and Amira were sharing—just a simple exchange of words, but the teaching of signs and sometimes sketches on the large note-pad they had balanced on their laps was letting Robyn into Amira's world. Showing her just how much the somber little girl understood and could communicate.

"I thought I'd show you things, items of interest, along the way," Idris grumbled. "But I can't get a word in edgewise with the two of you going on about camels and birds and who knows what else."

"If I didn't know better, I'd say you were jealous!" Robyn replied absently, eyes still on the drawing of a...was that a solar panel next to the waves?

"I am *not* jealous."

Robyn sat upright and looked into the rear-view mirror, her eyes just missing Idris's irritable glance. When his gaze returned to the mirror and meshed with her own, she saw a hit of *relief*. As if a mutual need for the other was confirmed within that brief moment. A need she hadn't yet acknowledged.

A heat grew in her belly and the atmosphere shifted from playful to taut as Amira, thankfully, remained deeply engrossed in her drawing.

Idris returned his focus to the road, but she could see from the stiffening of his shoulders he had felt it, too. The connection.

"It is tricky," Robyn began tentatively, "with Amira needing to read lips. I don't want her to feel left out." Idris's eyes remained focused on the road. He was leading a relatively impressive group of vehicles through the countryside. When he'd said Robyn could "raid the store cupboard" at the hospital she hadn't expected a warehouse.

"Of course," Idris replied stiffly as if that had been the point he'd been trying to make all along. "She is the reason you're here."

"Although—" a surge of chance-taking overtook her "—most children her age aren't all that interested in what adults yammer on about."

"Most children her age don't have a country to be responsible for."

"True." Robyn leaned forward, resting her arm on the back of the empty passenger seat. "If you're fishing for compliments about your daughter, I can tell you for free, she's exemplary."

"And the rest of your advice?" Idris's lips twitched with something. Pride? Humor? Or another streak of irritability she seemed to have a knack for tapping? "Does that come with a price tag?"

Robyn laughed. Whether he was annoyed or not she lived in a far different world to Idris and his bottomless coin purse. "If it's medical advice you're after, and I didn't need to pay my rent or eat, I would work at Paddington's for free. Especially if it meant keeping the doors open longer."

"Sounds like you mean it."

"I do! Being head of the surgical ward is—well, I don't so much like the public side of things, but helping the children, working with the children... It really is my passion."

"Even though—"

"Yes," she answered quickly. "It's hard sometimes, I admit, but..."

"And how about this move to the outskirts of London—"

"To Riverside Hospital?" It was hard to keep the derisive tone out of her words, but she was grateful for the change of conversation topic. Surprised, in fact, he'd brought it up at all.

"Yes." Idris nodded, eyes occasionally meeting hers in the rearview mirror as the city sights began drifting away and the road curved into an ever-increasing expanse of desert. "What would be so bad about moving there?"

"Everything!"

"Won't it have new facilities, new equipment?"

"It would be a soulless replication of what we have now. A business park of a hospital." *Just like that palace of yours—sitting empty in the middle of such a thriving city.*

"And the reason for the move?"

"The board wants to sell the site. It would," she

acquiesced with a sigh, "bring a lot more money to the hospital—but a lot of added expense for all of the patients and their families with the travel, the hotels." She pulled herself up short. "I feel like I'm giving a speech and that's not really my turf."

"No? It was sounding quite convincing to me."

This time she was certain he was smiling.

"I think speech making is more likely your terrain."

"When necessary," he conceded. "But this—" He drew his hand along the view spreading out before them as they crested a steep hill. "This is the terrain that sings to me."

Robyn was speechless. The capital city was on the sea and very beautiful, but the vast peninsula they were overlooking now was absolutely breathtaking. A huge sprawl of orchards and marshland and the most extraordinary coastline was spilling out beneath their hillside vantage point.

"No wonder…"

"No wonder what?" Idris asked.

"You're so passionate about Da'har. It's absolutely beautiful."

"No more so than—" Idris stopped himself short, forcing himself to tear his gaze away from Robyn for fear of betraying what he really wanted to say. That she was beautiful. Fiercely intelligent. Passionate about children when others in her shoes would have walked away.

Being with her brought life back to parts of him he'd long ago consigned to the past.

"No more dedicated than you are to Paddington's," he said instead.

"Birds of a feather, us two."

From Robyn's tight reply, he wished he'd just said what he'd meant to.

No more beautiful than you are.

Pretending he was unaffected by her beauty was increasingly difficult. He was beginning to wish he had selected one of the potbellied, middle-aged *male* surgeons who'd all but kowtowed to him for the honor of doing Amira's surgery. But Robyn?

She didn't kowtow. She didn't beg.

First impressions? A scatterbrained wood nymph. The more he grew to know her, the more he appreciated how right he had been to go with his gut. Much like him, she was a woman who didn't bother with charades. She was the best and didn't need to try to impress. It wasn't arrogance. It was simply the way it was. Her commitment, lauded skill and ability to help his daughter weren't the only factors at play.

He was *moved* by Robyn. She reached places in his heart he had slammed shut for good, and the thought of opening those doors, of letting himself love again? It was easier to imagine Amira being able to hear than envisioning himself happy and in love.

"What are those?" He followed the line Robyn's finger drew, catching glimpses through the side mirror of his little girl's face pressed up against the window, her eyes actively absorbing everything she saw. This was a first for her and he felt a twinge of remorse they hadn't done this earlier. That he'd opted to drive instead of sit alongside her and tell her his childhood tales of exploring the nooks and crannies of the fertile valley below them.

"It's a solar farm. For the orchards and farms," he explained.

"The orchards? I would've thought there was more than enough sun to ripen the crops."

"You're right on one count. We have more than enough sun, but not enough water. What you can't see, beyond the mountain range at the far end of the valley, is a desalination plant. We built it out of sight of the handful of villages that populate this valley as it is less than complementary to the rural setting. The electricity made helps pump the water from underground tunnels here into marshlands and into reservoirs for the orange groves and pomegranate orchards."

"It all sounds incredibly well thought out."

"These are the types of decisions I enjoy making," Idris said, surprised to hear the depth of feeling in his own voice.

"Did you study all of this? The hydro, the salination, solar-powered orchard-crafting?" Robyn laughed as she garbled the multilayered technologies, and he found himself chuckling along with her.

The team of engineers he'd worked with to put together the complementary power and hydration systems would've died of shock. It had been one of the first projects he had put together in the wake of his wife's death when he had been a shell of the man who had ascended to the throne. Where he had once felt there was nothing he couldn't overcome, he now saw what all those who came into contact with him must've spotted a mile off. A man embittered by life. Angry. Hollowed out by the cruel twist life had taken on an otherwise blissfully happy ride.

"You remember, of course, that I studied architecture in university," he explained. "I also took a higher degree in urban and rural planning. So much of the region—the Gulf Peninsula—is turning to desert faster than we can find ways to fight the loss of precious agricultural land. If farmers abandoned their crops and moved to the cities, we as a nation would be forced into an untenable position. My people must have food and water. The rest…?" He paused, eyes scanning the lush agricultural land below he played a key part in maintaining. But the swell of pride wasn't for himself. "I want Amira to have a country able to fend for itself when it is her turn to rule. A country that hasn't been savaged for its resources for my own gain without thought for the ramifications."

"That is very noble," she said, feeling deep in her heart that a man who cared this deeply was both generous and kind—no matter the steely exterior he presented to the world.

As if to prove her point she watched as his jaw clenched while an eyebrow arched in displeasure at her words.

"There is no nobility in it when there isn't a choice. It is the *responsibility* of a father to look after his daughter."

"I know, but I don't think you see Amira that way. As a responsibility." Robin's voice was softer now. A welcome whisper in his subconscious telling him what he already knew. He did it for love. A love he found difficult to show for fear of ever experiencing the pain he had endured seven years ago.

"Just as well," he said, his voice gruff with emotion. "We've a busy few days ahead of us. All of us."

His lips pressed and tightened—a cue to Robyn that the conversation was over. As she relaxed back into the deep seat of the luxury four-by-four, he inhaled the sweet meadow blossom scent her movement left behind.

For every part of him that wanted Robyn near, that enjoyed having her as a confidante, a friend, there was another very active, near brutal part of him that knew having her close was akin to stepping in quicksand. If he were to fall in love with Robyn Kelly, there would be no going back. She deserved nothing less than a man's entire heart and he didn't have that to offer.

His nation and his daughter had endured enough. His future would be a solitary one.

CHAPTER SEVEN

"HOLD OUT YOUR HANDS!"

Amira could hardly contain her giggles, while her father's face was a picture of fastidious concentration.

"This is your grandfather's secret technique. Pay close attention." He tightened his grip on the knife and made a final and sharp incision.

"Oh!" Robyn cried. "Careful."

"And they all come out. Quickly, your hands! Just like this!"

Amira and Robyn held their hands out as gem after gem of ruby-colored fruit cascaded into their open palms. She'd never seen such beautiful pomegranates, let alone picked them from a tree jeweled to the hilt with them.

"So." Idris closed his sharp pocketknife after swiping the blade along a few tree leaves and plucked a couple of seeds from Robyn's cupped hand. "What do you think?"

He popped them into his mouth, and as his eyes connected with hers, the sun-warmed scent of his body swirled around her like an aphrodisiac. Her gaze shifted from his dark eyes along the straight-as-an-arrow line of his nose and landed on his mouth, her own lips parting as she watched the tip of his tongue slip out to retrieve a drop of juice. She stood, mesmerized, as one of his teeth bit down on his lip until slowly, agonizingly, the fullness of it was released, the color intensified by the skid of tooth against his very full, very kissable mouth.

Everything about the moment screamed erotic: the warm orchard and ocean-scented evening air; stars pinging out against the ever-increasing darkness above the sea as the waves hushed and whooshed upon the sand, advanced and retreated. Advanced and retreated. Candles flickered in abundance inside the hurricane lamps dotted liberally about the "campsite" Idris's staff had set up for them three days into their journey.

An entire crescent of perfect beach, just for them! Bedouin-style tents with a luxury of mattresses, pillows... Everything she would have imagined an Arabian warrior would be privy to. The canopy-tented "living room," the solar-powered showers hidden by gently billowing canvases, the bed so large she could sleep on it diagonally without the slightest of concerns— none of these were set out to impress her. It was how the very real Sheikha-in-waiting and her father, the powerful and benign leader of all they had seen on their extraordinary trip to this seaside retreat, lived. Not ostentatiously, but it was undeniably luxurious.

She chanced another glance at Idris and was instantly snared by the intensity of his returned gaze. Unable to move, the only thing she could remember to do was breathe.

Was the pull of attraction mutual? The same type of magnetism that bound the moon, the earth and the sun. Utterly organic. Completely undeniable.

Her body had no resistance to fight the waves of desire being near Idris elicited. Proximity as he took a single step closer toward her only magnified the sensations, the tingles of response. His unblinking gaze, knowingly or not, was turning her very essence into a heated, molten pool of longing.

She lifted her hand, only just stopping herself from reaching out to caress the dark outline of his evening stubble when Idris quickly averted his eyes to remind her they weren't alone.

Amira, thankfully, was oblivious to their otherworldly moment brought on—no doubt—by too much time in the sun and not enough...

Not enough what? Common sense?

Probably.

Robyn sucked in a quick breath of air and plopped down on the rattan sofa awash with pillows, patting the space beside her for Amira to come and finish off the pomegranate seeds her father had prepared for her after another wonderful picnic dinner.

Idris took a seat across from them underneath the large, open tent his staff had arranged for them to enjoy their supper and the sunset.

Just as well, she chided. Amira was why she was here, not...not having *moments* with the last person on the planet she should be getting all swoony over. Not that she was swoony or anything. Not much, anyway.

"So." Idris eventually broke the silence, well aware something had passed between them. Something overtly sensual. "I suppose it's time for Amira to head to bed."

"Already?" Robyn's expression was slightly stricken as though she were planning on using his daughter as a shield to protect herself from being ravaged by him. The thought was far too easy to picture.

Robyn's golden curls splayed out on the rich colors of the throws and blankets that made up his bed. Her slender limbs moving, responding beneath him as he—

"Do you read to her?"

Idris's eyebrows furrowed together in near disbelief. "You do remember my daughter is deaf, Dr. Kelly?"

Robyn stiffened at the use of her formal title and he instantly regretted the patronizing tone he knew came too easily. More so when he saw his daughter was following the words being shaped by his lips.

Amira blinked, almost in confusion at the version of the father neither of them much liked. Cold. Unfeeling. Indifferent. All things he was most definitely not feeling now, but needed to fight.

Robyn saw the interchange and busied herself with scrubbing a wet wipe over Amira's hands, giving a kiss to each of her fingertips after it had been cleaned. She looked across to Idris when she gave Amira a wipe to do the same for her.

"Has anyone taught you how reading to the deaf needs to be a slightly different experience?"

He shook his head no. Communicating and educating his daughter was incredibly complex. He had, much to his shame, relied on the hope that one day the miracles of modern medicine would eradicate the need to explore all the various teaching techniques a deaf child required when his energies should have been spent on working with deaf educators—taking advantage of his daughter's quick and eager mind.

One look from Robyn and he felt disappointed in himself. As Robyn had said, the operation wasn't necessarily going to be successful. But he would empty the family's coffers to the very last coin if it would make it so.

"I have a book in my bag I think she might enjoy. The vocabulary might be a bit advanced for her reading level." Robyn's voice was neutral, but those amber eyes of hers spoke volumes.

This isn't about you, they said. *Your ego. Your hopes. This is about your daughter and her welfare. Right. Now.*

"Would you like to show us?"

The light he so enjoyed seeing returned to Robyn's eyes at his request.

"Very much." She thanked Amira for cleaning her hands, then explained what she wanted to do—sending the little girl to run and fetch the book.

"We could have sent someone." Idris felt the thunderclouds gather again.

"Children," Robyn said firmly, "enjoy helping. It makes them feel a part of things."

"I give her everything she needs."

"No one is saying otherwise." Robyn folded her hands together on her lap as if they would provide the calm she needed to keep her response in check. "Sometimes what a child needs more than *things* is to be *needed.*"

Idris sat back against the pile of scarlet and white pillows, wondering what had made this woman so strong. No one spoke to him like this.

Ever. And yet…they were all things he needed to hear. The voice of reason to the black-and-white view of the world he'd adopted after his wife had died.

"Here she is." He beckoned his daughter to come over and join him, wrapping a protective arm around her shoulders as she held the book up for Robyn to see.

"Great!" Robyn signed as she spoke in a steady clear voice. "Idris, if you wouldn't mind reading the story, I will sign along with my own narration. That way you can see the difference."

"Won't you just be repeating what I say?"

"Not exactly. Sign language isn't a word for word translation. It's more…" Her eyes flicked up to the soft billows of fabric hanging above them, the candlelight adding gold to the luster of her richly colored irises. "Signing a story is more often a case of capturing the essence of the tale, details when necessary, but a big mix of using your face and your expressions to tell the story, as well. Often in written language, so much is implied and, in this case, they need to be explained. Sometimes just using the pictures in the book along with a sign is helpful. Here, let me show you."

She crossed to where he and Amira were seated and sat next to him, her scent immediately causing him to lose focus and stiffen.

The entire reason he'd sat across from her was to shake off his body's unbidden response to Robyn, not compound it! And yet, her focus was entirely on Amira, the book he held in his lap and showing him, as he imagined she would show any parent trying to do the best by their child, how to read a story.

"So!" Robyn clapped her hands together and gave him a quick look. "Shall we begin? If you just start with the title."

"Beauty and the Beast," Idris read dryly. "I suppose you find that funny."

Robyn looked up at him, her face a picture of innocence and then began to sign. Her fingers widened as she fanned them across her face with a beatific expression in her eyes, then abruptly crumpled her face into a grumpy mirror image of his own, fingers curling in an angry twist in front of the face before she looked back at him with a grin.

"It's just a fairy tale. Don't be scared."

Idris gave her his best sidelong look. "Shall I continue?"

"Yes, please do. This is excellent fun!"

Much to his surprise, Idris did actually enjoy telling the story "Robyn-style." He read the story aloud, one line at a time, and Robyn would either repeat the line verbatim—particularly if it was about an action—or, if it was more subtle, she would explain it fully until Amira's eyes lit with understanding. Seeing Robyn's slender fingers spell things out alongside the pictures in the beautifully illustrated book and then take flight, usually up toward her face where her expressions alone told the tale of a young woman traded by her father in exchange for a single, exquisite rose by a hideous monster who was really a handsome prince cast under a spell for cruel, selfish behavior.

Idris, despite an inclination to slam the book shut at the constant flow of similarities, found himself engaged. He grew nearly as wide-eyed as his daughter when Beauty left the Beast behind only to discover him half-dead for grief at the loss of her and ultimately transformed into the handsome prince he had once had the chance to be.

"And that," Robyn said with a satisfied smile at the sight of her openmouthed audience, "is how you tell a story in sign language!"

"Very...persuasive." Idris chose his words carefully. It could just be coincidence that art was imitating life a bit too accurately. Who knew? Maybe that magic carpet bag of hers had an entire library of fairy tales and myths in it. Fiction. That was all it was, he reminded himself as his daughter's sleepy form began to press against him. "It's definitely time for this little one to get her beauty sleep." He scooped her up in both arms, Amira's long black hair swishing across his arm as he brought her forehead up to meet his lips for a kiss. As he dropped the kiss on his daughter's brow, he looked up just in time to catch a glimpse of Robyn's tear-filled eyes as she looked out to the sea, her hands wiping at her cheeks as she walked briskly out into the darkness toward the retreating tide.

"Are you happy with your tent?" he called after her. It was a ridiculous question. She'd been sleeping in the same high-caliber Bedouin-style tent for the past three nights they had been touring. It was every bit as luxurious as the palace. Tonight, however, with the glaze of tears in her eyes, he was vividly aware she would be on her own and he wanted, much to his surprise, to be with her. All of them. Just as he had with his extended family when they'd come to this very same beach when he was a child. The whole lot bundled into the extensive bedroom, telling stories, laughing, until one by one, eventually, they had all drifted off to sleep with the sound of the waves as their lullaby.

"Very," came the tight reply, shoulders stiffening at the realization she hadn't quite escaped his notice.

"I'll just put Amira down."

He saw her nod her head, working her way to

the shoreline, only the phosphorescence of the foam visible in the inky darkness now enveloping her.

"Here." Idris's voice broke into the still night air. "For the cold."

Robyn started as she felt a soft cashmere wrap being placed on her shoulders. She didn't need to turn to identify the voice or the fingers staying just a moment longer than she would have thought necessary to ensure the wrap would stay.

"Thank you for the story. Amira loved every moment of it."

"My pleasure." She kept her gaze straight ahead, somehow finding it just a bit too painful to look him in the eye. Not with everything she was feeling. The weightless, out of control, topsy-turvy journey that was falling in love. Because that was what was happening. Despite her very best efforts, she was falling in love with Idris. At least, with the man he was when he let his guard down. When he reveled in showing them the best way to open a pomegranate. When he tightened his grip on the steering wheel as he spoke of his country's transformation from tribal outpost to international stalwart on both financial and political fronts. The way his eyes lit when he looked first at his daughter and then, on occasion, at her.

What she couldn't bear was the wall she regularly saw slide into place when whatever it was that was happening between them grew too intense.

But he was right, wise even, to keep the wall between them strong. He belonged here. A modern-day knight for a country that needed a strong leader—someone unafraid to face the future on his people's behalf.

Robyn was half in love with the country, as well, but her place was at Paddington's. Behind the scenes. Doing what she did best beneath the harsh glare of the surgical lamps…

"Come." Idris tipped his chin toward the soft light of the tent. "Sit with me awhile."

"I should probably make a few calls. Check in with the hospital." She winced apologetically, backing away from the hand he'd held out to place on the small of her back.

He noticed the move but said nothing, folding his hands behind his back, as if he'd intended to do so all along.

"Actually…it's probably best we speak before you make that call."

Robyn's sense shot to high alert. "You don't want to cancel the surgery, do you?"

"No, no. Nothing like that." He shook his head and took a seat in an armchair, gesturing that she should sit on the sofa across from him while they spoke. "It's just, seeing you here, with Amira—

the both of you discovering what I love about Da'har so much—I'm beginning to think it would be best if we had the surgery here. She's had so much change already—"

Robyn's head was shaking no, no, no, before her mouth caught up with her. "I will only do the surgery at Paddington's. With great respect to you and your team, it's where I am most comfortable. Where I will be able to ensure I will do my best work."

"This is not what I want!" Idris slammed his fist against the wooden table sitting between them, the force behind his gesture so intense it sent the reverberations of his anger straight through to Robin's core.

She sat bolt upright and locked eyes with him. "Not everybody always gets what they want, do they, Your Excellency? As you yourself once said, life isn't fair."

The words furled out from her mouth like a whip—snapping with a ferocity she hadn't realized she'd possessed.

"You won't stop me from protecting Amira." Idris's voice was low, a near growl. "I have the power to stop this thing—whenever I choose."

And that was when she saw it clearly. The fear. The living terror that something would happen to his daughter and he would be powerless to change it. Her heart ached for him, but he had to see that micromanaging wasn't love. Trust and faith and courage—those were the fibers that made love strong.

She took a deep breath and looked him in the eye again.

"I owe Amira my absolute concentration in the operating theater. The one place she will receive that is Paddington's. You can't control everything, Idris. Least of all me. Perhaps it's time to focus on what you do have rather than what you don't."

"I have a daughter who can't hear!" His voice rose again.

"You have a loving, joyful, curious, amazing daughter who would do anything for you if only you'd let her."

He let the words sink in, his body visibly battling a need to vent his frustration.

"Can you promise me absolute success in Paddington's?"

"No," she said plainly. "But what I can promise is my very best."

Robyn's hands curled into fists to hide the tremors that would betray her to Idris.

He considered her silently for a moment, his body still taut with his ferocious need to protect his daughter. She felt naked beneath his gaze and it took all her courage not to look away. She wriggled some more strength into the line of her spine, all the while meeting the depths of his ebony eyes when running away would have been the easiest option.

"What is it?" Idris asked, his voice unexpectedly softening, teasing away the harshness of his steely-eyed expression. "What is it you didn't get that you wanted so badly?"

"A child," she said simply, her eyes bravely linked to his so he could see the truth in them. "A child of my own."

"You would be a wonderful mother." The words came without reservation and she felt them in her heart.

"Alas!" The corners of her lips tipped upward, parting with a bittersweet smile. "It is not to be."

"Do you mind my asking why not?"

She sighed, pressing her hands between her knees, hunching her shoulders up around her ears. "It's not a very nice story."

"Whatever it is, you've lived to tell the tale. Someone very wise once told me I should focus on the positive."

She arced an eyebrow at him. It wasn't strictly what'd she'd said, but it had been the message.

"I'm paraphrasing," he intoned with a gentle smile.

"Of course." She knew the smile she was offering him in return was wan, but she felt a strength growing in her. One that might lend a voice to her story.

She tipped her head and gave him a sidelong look. His expression wasn't as enraged as she might have expected after their fiery exchange. It was, in fact, one that spoke of a new understanding. Perhaps a realization that holding his daughter as tightly to him as he did could be restrictive rather than loving. That holding on to the grief and fear of the unknown that had come with his wife's death might be suffocating his heart and soul—rather than enlightening them.

Robyn tugged the edges of the shawl around her shoulders and tucked her feet up and under her on the cushioned sofa. She was going to have to get comfy if she was going to spill this particular pot of beans.

"You're difficult to say no to, you know."

"You're difficult in your own special way, but let's not worry about that now." Idris reached across and took one of her hands in his, his thumb giving her palm a few short rubs before releasing it and settling back in his chair. "Please. I want to know."

The candlelight flickered off the dark shine of his hair, but his black eyes were lit entirely from within.

"A little while ago," she began, then laughed softly before correcting herself. "A long time ago actually, since forty is looming out there."

"What? Forty looms for the both of us."

She couldn't help it. She snorted. "You're a whippersnapper at thirty-five."

"You can barely be into your thirties."

"Thirty-seven," she corrected, not a little pleased to see his eyes widen with genuine disbelief. Idris didn't do social niceties so she knew it had to be real. "Guess that makes you my boy toy!"

Oh, wow. Did you really just say that?

"Does it, now?" Bemused didn't even begin to cover the expression she received in return.

"Can we just forget I said anything?"

"Probably for the best," he conceded, a twinkle of humor coming to the fore.

"Anyhow—" she gave him a soft smile and a nod of thanks for wiping the slate clean "—when I was in my very early twenties, still in med school, I was in a relationship and fell pregnant."

"You were married?"

"No." She didn't meet Idris's gaze, her fingers busy toying with the tassels on the ends of the shawl he had placed protectively on her shoulders.

"Was he not an honorable man?"

She looked up, surprised to see the flare of protectiveness surge through him on her behalf.

"He was, but what happened to the two of us… it was tough." It surprised her how easy it was to speak to Idris. The man who seemed so solid, so absolute about his opinions—he wasn't sitting there, body taut with tension to judge her, but to defend her if necessary, and she hadn't felt that sort of security in, well, ever. The rest of the story came out in a whoosh of information. The medical school romance, the unplanned pregnancy. "I hadn't realized how much I had wanted a child until I was pregnant and John was a good guy so we thought, why not? Why not have a child?"

"So what happened?" Idris pressed, concern weaving through his voice.

And this was the hard part. "It was an ectopic pregnancy." She shot him a glance, and instead of feeling strange telling him about the intimate details, she felt relief. He didn't seem squeamish or put off. Just profoundly interested in what had happened to her to change her life so much that she would always feel a longing for something she could never have. She went on to tell him about the cervical pregnancy. The fetus had implanted so near her uterus it had sustained a gestational sac. She had known the chances of the baby surviving were rare, but abortion hadn't been a choice she'd wanted to make. There had been bleeding. Too much bleeding. And ultimately a hysterectomy to save her life, but not the life of her child.

"The ramifications of what had happened to me—to my body—were too much for John and we drifted apart. There was a job offer from Paddington's that lifted my heart out of the abyss and now it's just me and my work!" She put on the bright smile she was so accustomed to pasting on at moments like these. The ones where she wondered if she really had healed and moved on from that devastating day. There were no visible scars, but she would be in complete denial not to admit that the emotional fallout ran deep.

"I am so sorry, Robyn. You didn't deserve that."

"No one does," she quipped, pulling her hands back as she saw him come forward to offer her a comforting caress. Feeling his touch, the soft shift of his thumb along the back of her hand, along the length of her arm, would tip her over the edge, and this was a work trip. She might be great at giving advice, but taking her own seemed nigh on impossible.

"You know, I really do have to make a few calls to the hospital. Check up on how things are going." She pressed up from her chair and gave her legs an unnecessary brush for sand.

"Surely they would get in touch with you if they needed anything." Idris rose with her, his body language still hovering between his usual reserve and a newfound intimacy sprung from the fears and sorrows they had shared.

It was an intangible line the pair of them

could cross—a shared discovery of all the joy just waiting to fan out before them—if only life were so easy. Idris didn't want *her*. He wanted his daughter to hear. And he would do anything in his power to make it happen. So, Robyn did a quick internal round of shutting the doors to everything she'd laid bare before him and gave Idris a bright smile.

"There are a few things I wanted to make sure are under way as regards Amira's surgery. If we're still green-lit, that is?" She crossed her arms protectively, the delicate fabric of the shawl between them a reminder their futures were linked now…at least professionally speaking. And that was the part she needed to secure.

"Very well."

Robin watched as the shutters slammed shut in Idris's eyes. His lips pressed tightly together to form a straight line as the cool, icy distance she'd felt the very first time they met sent shivers along her spine.

Again, she knew sleep would be some time coming and, when it did, there was little mystery as to who would haunt her dreams.

CHAPTER EIGHT

As dawn broke Idris squinted against the sun's glory while it crested the mountain peaks encircling the valley and seaside cove where their camp lay. He stretched and pushed himself up and out of the tangle of bedsheets that hadn't seen much sleep, elbows coming to rest on his knees, fingers templing, thumbs pressing into his brow as he sat in a contemplative silence he hoped would bring some peace.

Restlessness won out. He tugged on a pair of swimming trunks hoping a long swim could achieve what his normally very controlled mind could not. He slipped his feet into his sandals, aligning the tan lines with the bands, suddenly appreciating how much he had been in "holiday" mode for the past few days. Traveling with Robyn and his daughter had been something he hadn't experienced for a while. Years, in fact. It had been…fun.

Very much like the childhood his parents had ensured he'd had. Not at all similar to the one he afforded Amira.

He rounded the corner of his three-sided tent

only to find a very anxious-looking Robyn nibbling away on her tidy manicure, twisting her slender body this way and that in the loose confines of a light cotton dress. The spaghetti string straps gave a clear view of her slender shoulders and the soft swoop and curve toward her breasts. No brassiere or bikini straps, just two triangles of cloth forming an eye-catching V in the center of her décolletage.

The traditional clothing she'd been wearing had never afforded him so much... *Robyn*...and there was no denying he liked what he saw. She turned and noticed him watching.

Unable to look away, he shifted his gaze along the soft arc of her breasts, her nipples tightening against the thin cotton as if he had reached out and caressed them between a finger and thumb or given them a swift lick with his tongue. A shot of desire slammed through him as the possibilities developed and grew. There was no one around at this hour. His tent was bathed in the apricot and gold light only a Da'harian sunrise could elicit. His fingers twitched, each hand longing to play its part in separating Robyn from her dress. Not by the gentle slipping of one strap and then the next in a slow, luxurious unveiling, but with a sharp, brusque rent of the flimsy fabric so that he could see all of her at once, then decide slowly, luxuriously, where and how he would begin to touch and caress her naked body.

He surprised himself by taking a step forward. Just as quickly he ground his heels into the sand and his jaw into a tight clench, mind dictating to matter that he needed—he must—keep his primal response to her in check.

"You seem to have been lying in wait. I can only assume it was for me?"

Idris knew he sounded more growly than he would have liked, but he didn't like losing control and the unbidden jags of longing that just looking at Robyn unleashed in him needed to be tamed.

Her eyes widened with a combination of relief and nerves, both quickly evolving into something altogether different as he watched her eyes slip from his face and down to his bare torso.

Electricity crackled through him again as her lips parted and she unconsciously licked her lips before shifting her heavy-lidded gaze upward to meet his. Her hands dropped to her sides and whatever it was that had been disturbing her seemed to have left her completely as she opened and closed those rose-red lips.

"Care to join me for a swim?"

It wasn't a request. He needed to get in the deep, cool seawater. Now.

"Ah, no, it is—rather, that is, I was—" she stammered out a few false starts.

"Come on. Spit it out." He reached into his tent and grabbed a towel, wrapping it around his waist to increase the divide between them.

"The press have got hold of the news."

His focus swung from lust to protective in an instant.

"About Amira?"

"About the surgery, yes."

"What calls did you make last night?"

"I rang the hospital. Paddington's." Her brow crinkled into tight furrows of concern.

"Who did you speak with?"

Robyn held her hands up in protest as he approached. "Please. No, Idris. I'm so sorry. I only spoke to one of my colleagues about where to place the 3-D printer and—"

"Word leaked out," he finished for her, arms crossing over his chest as he tried to put the information into some sort of order before he spoke again.

Robyn nodded somberly, rubbing her thumb again and again across the palm of her other hand as if it would expel the nerves that roller-coastered through her gut. If he decided to withdraw consent for the surgery now, the future of Paddington's could only be closure. Coming to Da'har had been scary enough. Now she was going to have to well and truly fight to save the one thing that meant the most in the world to her.

She could virtually see the thoughts flicking through Idris's eyes as he dismissed option after option. She'd told him to loosen the reins of control and *wow*! What a backfire.

A sudden clap of his hands jolted her to attention.

"First things first, I'll cancel the visit to Amaleet today."

"To see the children singing and the hawk display?"

She received a curt nod, a distracted glance.

"What on earth for? The press won't be there, surely! Amira was so looking forward to being with the other children."

Was she defending Amira or Paddington's? Had the futures of both become equally important? Robyn's hand moved instinctively to her heart.

"We'll go another time, when the children aren't there," Idris continued, his statement making little to no sense.

Was he wrestling with his need to control everything? This sort of thing—a media leak— was precisely what he wouldn't want for Amira. Robyn, of all people, understood the desire for privacy. The fact news of the surgery would be hitting all of the British newspapers at dawn made her sick. For herself, the promises she'd made to Idris of absolute privacy and, most worryingly, for the future of Paddington's.

Robyn watched as he shifted his jaw from left to right as if tasting the results of his decision. "Perhaps, if we cancel the other children she can see the hawk display."

"Don't you think she wants to do these things with other people? The same way you experienced them as a child."

"It's safer for her this way. Easier."

"Amira's deaf, not agoraphobic!" Robyn protested.

"And Amira's my daughter, not yours."

If he had slashed her with a knife the words could not have cut deeper.

She took a step back, barely able to contain the slug of grief rising in her throat.

Idris was drawing his line in the sand—in concrete more like—and Robyn would have to respect it. She'd promised him privacy and had landed him on the front page.

She swallowed all the things she could have said. All the feelings near enough choking her as she widened her tearless eyes. She may have fallen at this hurdle, but would not give Idris the satisfaction of seeing her cry.

"In which case, it's best I return to England.

I've spent enough time with you," she added hastily.

She was going to have to have a talk with her "out-loud" voice.

"I think you'll agree it's probably best if I got back to Paddington's and began organizing things. Particularly under the circumstances."

"No. You will stay in Da'har," Idris replied, his temper barely contained. "As discussed."

Forcing on a braver face than the one she knew it was masking, she, too, pressed her heels into the sand for better grounding and drew a deep breath before jabbing an accusing finger in his direction.

"I know you are Amira's father, but either our talk last night meant absolutely nothing to you, or you are suffering from a rather severe case of floccinaucinihilipilification." She sucked in another breath, feeling her confidence whoosh out of her with the word she'd summoned from only heaven knew where. An attack of Englishness forced her to tack on, "If you don't mind me saying."

"I'm not certain I know *what* it is, let alone if I'm suffering from it." Idris arced an imperious eyebrow. Something, Robyn now knew, he only did when his curiosity was piqued.

Ha!

"The action or habit of estimating something as worthless," she explained with a sniff.

"In other words, dismissing the opinions of others?" The eyebrow lifted again.

"Well…" She etched a heart shape into the sand with her toe. "I'm not *entirely* sure if I would have put it precisely as you did. But yes." She raised her eyes to meet his, surprised to find Idris smiling.

"I'm not so sure you are as shy of asserting yourself as you profess, Dr. Kelly."

"Robyn," she gently corrected, a warm hit of pride tickling at her heart as she spoke.

"Very well, then. I won't cancel the day's events. We carry on as—" Idris paused to give her a conciliatory smile "—as the doctor ordered."

Robyn's smile flattened into a grimace.

"Why the frown? You just got what you wanted, my dear. Usually a victor smiles."

Robyn cinched her lips back into a facsimile of a smile. "This isn't about winning or losing, Idris. It's about what's best for your little girl. If you would just hang up the 'underaged curmudgeon badge' you so proudly wear you might be able to see sense for once!"

"Underaged curmudgeon?"

"Yes." She gave him an indignant little nod. "You're far too young and gorge—" She swallowed the rest of her sentence and started again. "You're far too young and gifted a leader to be this grumpy. It's usually Victorian gentlemen with gout who are this consistently horrid."

"You think I'm horrid?"

"I...might. Just a little," she squeaked, fingers held up in a tiny pinch, as her lungs strained against the huge breath she'd sucked in realizing she was about to tell him what she really thought.

And what she really thought was that underneath the thick layer of defensiveness there was a kind, loving father. A generous and thoughtful leader. A man whose capacity to love had... She was struck with an unexpected hit of disappointment that he had chosen never again to be open to the pure, enriching love between a man and a woman.

"You're right." Idris gave her a begrudging nod.

"About the gout?"

"Don't be ridiculous. I'm as healthy as an ox." He struck a pose and only released it when he was quite sure Robyn had appreciated quite how healthy he looked. Just as quickly his entire demeanor transformed into a businesslike mode. "We'll hold a press conference. *You* will, that is. We shall organize it at the television station back in the capital when we return. For now we will complete our trip. As scheduled."

Idris's eyes twinkled, his chin tilting to the right, lips pressing forward and that eyebrow of his arching in a self-satisfied sort of way.

Which was great, except… She raised her hand as if she were a girl back in school needing to ask for permission for something to which she already knew the answer was no.

"Is there any chance we could skip the press conference part?"

"Not even a sliver of a chance." He squared himself to her, arms crossing over the broad expanse of caramel-colored chest she'd fastidiously been trying to avoid staring at, as if crossing his arms put an end to the matter. And for the moment, it did, because the gesture near enough short-circuited her brain again. It wasn't so much the soft whorls of dark hair around the burnt-sugar areolas, but the arrow of hair between his taut stomach muscles and his hip-skimming swimming trunks. All a bit much in the visual overload department. Particularly when her mind needed to be one hundred percent focused on sorting out this PR palaver.

"What if you were to release a statement, or even deliver the statement?" she posited. "Surely people are more interested in what *you* have to say…"

"I think you will find, Dr. Kelly," Idris dryly replied, "it is your surgical skills and medical prowess the people are curious about. It would get you the much-needed publicity I am sure Paddington's requires in the face of this financial uncertainty. Come now—what was it you said I was suffering from earlier?"

"Floccinaucinihilipilification?"

"Yes. Let's not hope it's catching now, shall we?"

Her mouth went dry and she felt a funny, tickly, scratchy sensation in her throat. The same one that always threatened to squeeze her larynx into oblivion whenever the thought of speaking publically started worming its way through her nervous system. So she'd been the pot calling the kettle black. So what? This whole thing was about Idris and Amira—not about her!

"Couldn't we just use some of your gazillions and get ourselves a body double to do it for me?" she said, only half joking now that the words were out.

Idris's lips tweaked upward a couple of times before he drew them in and released them after a drag beneath his teeth. "*Gazillions* isn't a word I tend to use in reference to my wealth."

"Apologies." She fluttered her hands between them as if it would erase what she'd said and huffed out a defeated sigh. "I just…oh! This is so embarrassing since you're so good at it, but I absolutely, positively, couldn't find anything in the world more terrifying than giving a press conference."

Idris leaned his weight back on one foot and gave her a sidelong look. "Even when the future of Paddington's is at stake?"

"You're not threatening me, are you?"

"Not in the slightest. I'm just saying this is a news leak we need to harness. Gain control. You know I don't like it when things are out of my control and I know you will do anything to save Paddington's. I think it might be time to take a spoonful of your own medicine, Robyn."

As he spoke, his eyes raked across her and for the second time that morning she felt her body respond to his visual caresses. Her breasts pressed up against the brushed cotton of her overworn dress. Something she'd thrown on for an early-morning walk along the shoreline as she fought for the right way to explain to Idris that she'd lost control of the ship she hadn't been steering all that well in the first place.

"If it's all right, I'd like to think about it."

"Think about what you'll say?"

"Think about whether or not I'll do the press conference," she corrected, knowing the wince crinkling her nose and shooting her eyebrows up to her hairline wasn't really giving her the in-charge-of-the-situation look she'd been going for. Her teeth bit down on her lower lip too hard, too fast, and as she ran her fingers along the lip to feel for blood, she knew if she looked up, her cheeks would once again burn with response at being the object of Idris's heated looks.

"What if I agree to do it with you?"

Her eyes shot up, her fingers stilling along her lip as an injection of hope surged through her. "Really? You'd do that for me?"

"I'd do it for Paddington's."

Idris knew damn well he was offering to do the press conference for Robyn, but telling her so would be akin to opening a vault whose doors were already bulging with unshared revelations.

Unwittingly, Robyn was bringing him back to life. She enabled him to see the blessings he had instead of focusing on all those he didn't. She was of the simple-pleasures school of life and it was serving him well to have her remind him of the importance of them. He turned at the gentle shift in the wind and inhaled the sweet scent of a woman.

Robyn was growing increasingly uncomfortable underneath the weight of Idris's gaze as he absorbed the impact she'd made on, not just him, but his daughter, too. He'd rarely heard Amira laugh before, and now—he cocked his ear upward—he could make out the giggly laugh only a tickling session with her nanny might elicit. A tickling session the nanny would never have attempted before Robyn.

"Good. Well, then, if you'll excuse me, I'm off for a swim." He untucked the towel from his hips and swung it over his shoulder as if the entire matter were settled.

"We'll carry on with our tour of Da'har as scheduled, and in three days' time, we will give a press conference. If you could let the appropriate parties know, I would be grateful."

He strode away, a smile on his lips as he felt her turn her head to watch as he strolled off into the morning surf. He liked having her here and was loath to think of a life without her in it. In some capacity.

Perhaps, he mused, his lips quirking back up into a grin, his "gazillions" could help secure Paddington's future, freeing her up for periodic visits to Da'har. Amira would love to see her again. He was sure of that and he—

Idris stepped into the sea and took a sure-footed dive into the incoming waves.

Yes.

He would like that very much, as well.

It was incredibly difficult to fume when all Robyn was feeling was abject terror.

A press conference? In front of...*press*?

Five hours, a car ride across the mountains toward Da'har's central desert region and a breath-takingly delicious lunch hadn't done a jot to dissipate the growing panic over what she knew she had to do. A lunch of cardboard cutouts would most likely have done the same trick. And yet, the publicity the innovative surgery could generate was too important for the hospital to refuse. It was the whole reason she'd agreed to this hare-brained trip.

Her eyes flicked across toward Idris.

Well.

Mr. Tall, Dark and Sheikhy may have had something to do with it, as well. But it had *definitely* started with a Paddington's Only remit, she assured herself. No romance here. Not in this heart!

She glanced across at Amira—right up front near the falconry experts, the sun glinting off her dark hair, happy as a lark in the center of a whole gaggle of children despite Idris's earlier protests. She felt a smile twitch and form. She'd won that discussion, anyway.

This moment made the soul-digging glares Idris had scorched into her psyche worth it. Amira was giggling away and pointing, the children making up their own sign language on the spot to explain everything. Sign language that involved lots of jumping and soaring arms, hands turning into beaks snapping up unsuspecting prey.

Knowing how much more Amira could enjoy the interaction if she could hear, especially later when the children would sing for her, Robyn just had to perform the surgery.

Which meant…she would have to do the press conference.

She squeezed her eyes shut against the falconry display and willed the images of popping flashbulbs and whirring cameras to disappear. Did photographers even use flashbulbs anymore?

Her lids flew open again, squinting sharply against the glare of the late-afternoon sun.

"Aren't you enjoying the display?" the increasingly familiar voice rumbled into her ear, his scent wafting and twirling around her as he leaned in to demand her full attention. If they hadn't been all alone in the shaded viewing tent she might have— What? Might have fled? Kissed him? Laid herself out on the pile of cushions and cried, *Take me now!*

A twirl of heat took hold below her belly and she squelched the wickedly, sensual thoughts from her mind as best she could.

She gave him a quick smile and nodded. The part of her that was able to focus *was* really enjoying herself. Two men in traditional dress were riding bareback on a pair of ridiculously beautiful chestnut stallions. The falcons rode, perched on the leather tether strapped to each man's forearm, flying upward toward the blinding light of the sun, then spiraling downward when they caught the prey other men sent heavenward in catapults designed for the show. It was a huge blur of color, action and raw strength.

"Perhaps you'd like to see me in action?"

Idris's eyes were still on the display, but had that been a note of hope in his voice? Her jaw dropped. Was he *flirting* with her?

Too easily she could picture him in one of the loose silk tops, the center slit of the cobalt blue fabric bearing down the length of his midriff. She could practically see the cloth fluttering behind him as he galloped, exposing the golden expanse of his bare chest and stomach. A heated bolt of attraction crackled down her spine, pooling luxuriously below the waistline of her silken *sherwal*, despite frowning most sternly against the sensation.

Not good. Her body's response to merely *thinking* about Idris's naked torso told her she'd need to chain herself to a tent pole in order to resist leaning forward for just a teeny-tiny touch. Precisely the reason she should have stayed at Paddington's in her scrubs and working instead of coming to this wonderland that brought such light and…frisson to Paddington's most generous benefactor.

"A display may put us slightly behind schedule, of course." Idris's voice went slightly gravelly as he continued. "Riding in this heat is sweaty work."

Another burst of warmth showered through her at the thought of Idris standing beneath a cascade of water heated by the desert sun.

The inside of her cheek took a punishing blow as she tried to bite away the vision. She'd already had to scurry away once this morning when he'd strode off into the sea, knowing that watching him emerge from the water with that bronzed body, all dappled with drops of water, glistening in the morning sun...*agh!* Too much stimuli for her to compartmentalize.

Particularly with this blinking awful press conference hanging over her head.

"Don't worry about riding just for me. I'm fine."

Robyn shook her head in a solid "no" against the offer, but when a laser shot of disappointment streaked through Idris's dark eyes, she did an about-face so quickly she almost made herself dizzy.

"Now that I think about it... Yes. Absolutely, yes. I would love to see you in one of those shirts astride one of the stallions—"

She only just managed to stop midflow, a little too aware she had just opened her private thoughts to inspection.

Idris's lips, sensual beasts that they were, twitched forward, almost into a pucker. First a smile, then a frown was formed, and she couldn't help feeling like a starstruck teen as her heart began thumping in sporadic thuds, all but lurching straight up into her throat as she awaited his response.

"You wouldn't want to deny Amira a chance to see her father's prowess with a horse, would you? Maybe you'd inspire her to take up riding," she lamely tacked on, knowing her craving to see Idris at his rugged, shirtless, stallion-riding apex was a request best left unfulfilled.

"Of course," Idris answered, his features, as they most often were, recomposed into something unreadable even in the broad light of day. "My daughter has often told me she'd like to see me bare my chest to the elements, taking a horse under my command, teasing it into submission."

Robyn's eyes widened, then narrowed. "I do believe, Your Excellency, you are playing with my mind."

"Well spotted, Dr. Kelly."

She dipped into a small curtsy, and lowered her gaze. When she tilted up her head and dared to meet those black eyes of his, it was as if the invisible pane of glass between them had disappeared. The pounding of horses' hooves on the dunes accompanied the rhythm of her heart as Idris took her hand in his and raised it to his lips, eyes glued to hers as he pressed his mouth to the back of her hand.

Fireworks didn't even begin to cover her body's response to Idris's touch.

Feeling his lips upon her skin sent undulating waves of yearning through a bloodstream she was sure had been running on idle until Idris's kiss slammed it into high gear.

Idris let go of Robyn's hand as spontaneously as he had brought it to his lips, hoping to consign the action to a moment of madness, knowing full well the moments leading up to it had been laden with intent.

"I'm going to check on Amira."

He could feel Robyn's eyes on his back as he took the swift, long-legged strides he needed to work off whatever alchemy she had unwittingly bestowed on him. He'd thought the relationship he'd had with his wife was a once-in-a-lifetime experience. Now he knew he was wrong.

Robyn had found an entire fistful of keys with which to open his heart—door after door of revelation. And it simply wouldn't do.

He had a kingdom to run. A daughter's welfare to look after. A future… His breath caught as he thought of the instant and unfillable void that would be left in his life when Robyn went back to London. In their lives.

He shook off the scowl as he approached his daughter and placed his hands upon her slight shoulders. The children all turned to face him, their expressions suddenly somber, eyes wide as saucers as they looked upon their leader.

It was decision time. He felt Amira twist out of his hands and look up to him. She knew as well as he did this wasn't "normal." Playing with children as if she were just any old child. But she wasn't a regular. She would one day be responsible for the future of the very children she was playing with.

And he wouldn't have her embarrassed by the singing display he knew was coming next. These sorts of displays could wait until after the surgery.

He stretched his neck, hearing the tension kink and pop as he did. The surgery that was dependent upon Robyn. He would have to do his utmost to ensure it went ahead—no hitches.

"The musicians have asked us to go to the tent for the singing." Kaisha appeared by his side, her tone ever neutral.

"No." He shook his head firmly, giving Amira's head an apologetic stroke as he did. "It was mostly for Robyn's sake, but—"

"What was for my sake?" Robyn asked, tucking her headscarf protectively around her shoulders. The deep green of the scarf had shimmers of gold woven through it, adding luster to her amber eyes. He resisted the urge to get lost in them, putting on the blinkers that had seen him through the last seven years.

"Singing. If you really want to hear them sing, we can organize it back at the palace after Amira has gone to bed. I don't want her to be embarrassed."

"Why would she be embarrassed?"

"You, of all people, shouldn't have to ask that question." Idris felt his fingers tighten protectively around his daughter's shoulders.

"There are some wonderful ways to interpret music," Robyn protested, quickly kneeling down in front of Amira. "How would you like to hear your daddy sing to you?"

"You're just being cruel!" Idris protested in a low voice. "Why ask a question like that so close to the surgery? Of course she'd like to hear my voice. All of our voices, but she can't."

"No." Robyn looked up, her blond curls already escaping the confines of her scarf. "It's not cruel. It's realistic." She began signing as she spoke. "Your father is going to sing his favorite folk song to you." Then she fixed him with her eyes, a spark of defiance flaring in them as she did. "Get thinking. We've got to tell the musicians what they're about to play."

Enta eih.

Who was this woman? Powerful goddess or stubborn mule? For a split second Idris was grateful his daughter couldn't hear when he muttered a word not fit for any ears.

A bustle of activity ensued as, with Kaisha's help, Robyn scuttled everyone up to the open-sided tent prepared for the performance. He set off after her, his hand easily encircling her wrist as he pulled her around to face him.

"What is it you think you are doing? Public humiliation? Is that what you want for Amira?"

"How dare you!" she shot back. "How dare you think for a single moment I would do that to Amira."

"Then why do this? She is deaf!"

"Not for long if I have anything to do with it, and as such, she needs to be used to the same lives you and I are lucky enough to lead."

"What?" He couldn't keep the sneer from his face. "A life dedicated to nothing but work?"

She turned away, for just a moment, as if he had slapped her. After scraping her chin along her shoulder, she faced him again, the tiniest of twitches appearing at the corner of her eye. "I meant living a life where it is far too easy to take the most precious of gifts for granted."

Idris didn't have to ask her what she meant. He saw it all in her eyes. The same longing he felt.

The same struggle to break free from the locks and chains they'd imprisoned themselves with after grief struck in cruel, body-numbing blows.

"Sing to your daughter. I'll interpret."

It wasn't a plea. It was an entreaty to do the right thing.

Complex emotions poured into his heart, threatening to drown out his ability to think, let alone remember the words to a simple folk tune.

He'd never sung to Amira. Not once. And the understanding of that simple deprivation struck him hard. He'd been so busy protecting his child from what he thought would harm her, he had denied her the simple connections a parent and child could share. He grimaced and swallowed the strong sting of emotion at the back of his throat. Yet another thing he'd never succumbed to since his wife had died.

A few minutes later, at Robyn's suggestion, Idris was holding his daughter in his lap. Robyn stood across from him alongside the musicians and the children who had climbed onto a small set of risers.

"Whenever you're ready." Robyn nodded, almost too frightened to breathe. She could barely believe Idris had consented to her idea, let alone taken on board the all-too-real fact that she'd *vol-*

unteered to stand in front with the performers. But this was important.

Idris and Amira would have a steep learning curve to climb as the little girl entered the world of the hearing, and the closer the bonds they shared, the easier going forward would be. Her own childhood was woven together by her mother's lullabies and she couldn't imagine Amira not knowing the sensation of being sung to.

Robyn closed her eyes against Idris's unblinking gaze and imagined herself back in the London theater where she and Amira had first met. She'd signed for her then. This would be no different.

The moment the music began Robyn knew she'd vastly underestimated how different this scenario was. Her hips began to organically shift and move in time to the music—the handful of unfamiliar instruments transforming the space around them as if they'd taken a magic carpet ride to a different time and place. The collective sound of the children's voices thickened and swelled into one perfect voice and her eyes locked with Idris's as he, too, began to sing. His attention was wholly undivided. The words sung in Da'harian by the children, English by Idris, were being sung directly to her.

The lyrics of the song, while simple, were heartfelt and pure. They told the story of a poor shepherd boy who'd fallen asleep beneath a pomegranate tree, dreaming of the girl he hoped to marry when he made his riches from the flock who grazed around him.

Robyn signed the words; her body's movements encapsulated the rhythm and pacing of the music. Idris's rich baritone would be vibrating from his chest through to his daughter's back—a sensation every bit as powerful as hearing the song would one day be. It cinched her heart tight to see his daughter pull his arms tight around her as the drama of the story unfolded.

Translating became more intuitive as the song's journey through the young shepherd's imaginings built and unfolded. Robyn's eyes moved between Idris and Amira, her fingers flying to tell the unchecked dreams of the solitary young man. His hope that he'd one day be brave enough to ask the questions lying in wait upon his lips. It became impossible to separate the lyrics from the man singing before her.

Her body felt alive with possibility. Was she being serenaded? Was Idris telling her what she was only just realizing she felt for him? Was he telling her he loved her, too?

A surge of happiness threatened to split her heart in two as Amira, in the midst of a powerful drumming sequence, leaped to her feet, pulling her father up by both hands, and began to dance. Idris willingly complied, singing the chorus at full volume, his head thrown back as he scooped up his daughter and they twirled and spun to the hypnotic beat of the music.

When the cadence of the music slowed and the children's voices lifted softly in sync with the instruments, Idris shifted his daughter to his hip, her small hand on his heaving chest, both of their eyes solidly on Robyn as she interpreted the final chorus Idris had now begun.

The shepherd, Idris sang, was jarred from his sleep when a fruit fell from the tree. The thud of the pomegranate upon the ground woke him from a perfect dreamworld only to discover all of his sheep had gone and he was left with nothing but the sour scent of the broken fruit spoiling in the heat of the burning sun.

The music dwindled away and Robyn was left standing, her body frozen, as if she herself were caught between the conflicting worlds of hope and reality.

Amira's fingers were skating across Idris's lips and he pressed them to his daughter's small fingertips, giving them each a small kiss, his eyes still very much linked to Robyn's, his chest sucking in breath after life-affirming breath.

She turned abruptly, no longer able to stand in the remains of the words Idris had sung. Was it love he was feeling? Had it been love she'd seen in his eyes?

Or had he been trying to tell her what was inevitable? That theirs was a relationship never to be realized. Or worse. He could be telling her everything she'd thought had passed between them over the past week had all been in her head and there had never been any love at all.

CHAPTER NINE

"Dr. Kelly should be in the center," Idris directed the men setting up the nametags on the table, all the while looking over his shoulder to see where on earth she had got to.

"Are you sure?" Kaisha shot him a worried look and he didn't blame her.

They had spent large chunks of the past two days in the hospital at Robyn's request as she drilled the details of the surgery into her head.

He glanced at his watch. Twenty minutes until they would be live. Members of the press were already lurking outside the hospital doors. Some, he suspected, may have already wheedled their way in.

He and the press already had an...*understanding*. They left Amira out of the limelight, and he didn't shut down their businesses. He was all for democracy, but he valued privacy much, much more.

Where on earth was she?

He rocked back on his heels and worked his way through the past forty-eight hours. His eyebrows lifted in a satisfied arch as the answer came to him.

Sure enough, a few moments later he caught a glimpse of Robyn's tangle of blond curls hidden behind the foliage of an untamed succulent in the far corner of the central courtyard—a tiled maze of fountains, flower gardens and palms where patients and their families could escape the more sterile environment inside the hospital.

"Feeling up to facing your adoring public?" He sat down on the long slab of mahogany she was perching on, a clutch of note cards in her hands.

Robyn barked out a short laugh. "If I could hide back here and use a secret microphone, it would be much better."

He nudged her gently with his elbow. "You know you're up to it. Even Amira could talk you through the surgery at this point you've practiced on her so much."

"Would she like to do it? The press conference?"

He widened his eyes and gave her a very solid, "No."

Robyn turned to him, an embarrassed smile playing on her lips. "I've been horrible, haven't I?"

He lifted up his fingers and left a couple of centimeters between his thumb and index finger. "Just a bit horrible. The rest…" Their eyes clicked and with the connection along came the surge of endorphins he experienced whenever they shared a moment. "The rest of you has been *tolerable*."

Liar.

She swatted away his hand and laughed, for real this time. "You should be the one who's nervous."

"Why would I be nervous?" he riposted. "I have chosen the best surgeon for the job." He meant it, too. The more Robyn fine-tuned her explanation of the groundbreaking treatment, turning the complicated medical language into layman's speak, the more confidence he had in her abilities to give his daughter the gift of hearing.

He still couldn't shake the incredible feeling of dancing with Amira in his arms, singing at top volume, his daughter's hands pressed on his chest as he sang, her eyes glued to his lips, absorbing the story he told as actively as any hearing child might. It was a moment any father and daughter would have been lucky to share. For that alone, he owed Robyn an unpayable debt of gratitude.

The buzz of her phone broke into the shared silence his comments had brought and she shot him an apologetic smile as she dug, like a sorceress, into the depths of her bag and retrieved her mobile.

"Message," she said, her lips tightening as her eyes scanned the note.

"Everything all right?"

"No," she answered tightly. "One of the patients I was hoping wouldn't need to be readmitted has just been brought in."

"Anything I can do?" Idris offered inanely, but seeing the color drain from Robyn's cheeks showed him just how much she cared and he didn't like the helpless feeling it elicited.

"Not unless you've got a secret stash of millions you don't need," she replied, her thoughts clearly elsewhere.

She'd obviously meant it as a throwaway comment. Robyn had never asked him for a single thing. She was still trying to offer him money for the clothes they had bought at Amira's insistence, some of which she was wearing now.

The ensemble she'd chosen for the press conference was a beautiful sky blue, enhancing the rich coloring of her eyes, the soft pink of her lips and, now, the growing pink flush on her cheekbones as she became aware of the intensity of his gaze.

He shook his head and gave her knee a perfunctory pat.

"The best thing you can do for this patient—"

"Penelope," Robyn filled in.

"The best you can do—we can do—for Penelope is get on with this press conference. Bring the publicity you and your team deserve at Paddington's."

Robyn nodded. "I know. I just really can't bear all the attention. It genuinely terrifies me."

"Don't be scared." Idris, against his better judgment, took her hands in both of his and held them tight. "You were there for Amira and me yesterday in a way no one has been before. Today we are here for you."

The look she gave him in return was so filled with gratitude he had to fight not to pull her to him, holding her close as he had done once before.

With members of the press lurking everywhere it made things more complicated. The last thing he wanted was photos giving the wrong impression of their relationship taking precedence over the press conference. He could see the headlines now: *Royal Scandal! Passion Not Parenting!*

If only they knew how incredible a parent Robyn would be to his little girl. Their instant connection, the smiles, the *laughter*! Amira would be hard-pressed to find someone else to better fill the space her mother had left in her wake.

Idris's chest instantly hollowed as the air swept out of his lungs.

A mother for Amira.

She had a mother!

A mother she'd never known. Never would.

Robyn offered…possibility.

He looked down at Robyn's fingers, nervously tip-tapping against his hands, and swallowed away the conflicting thoughts. With a sharp breath, he placed her hands back in her lap, wishing he'd never taken them up at all. Robyn didn't need any diversions. Nor did he.

"Come." He rose and tipped his head toward the lecture room where everything had been set up for them. "Leave that enormous bag of yours and let's go dazzle the media."

An anxious smile crept onto Robyn's lips. "You'll be in the room, right?"

A simple question, but the look in her eyes was so much more complex. The only thing he could think of in response to the hope alight in those amber eyes of hers was, *As long as you need me, I'll be there.*

The words were still ringing in Robyn's ears as she settled herself into the chair at the center of the table. "As long as you need me, I'll be there."

She was beginning to think forever might be just about long enough, but she would take right now as a starting block. She'd seen something in Idris's eyes just then. Something she knew a glance in the mirror would reveal in her own.

Love.

She loved him. She loved Amira. Heck! She loved Da'har with its varied landscape, the rich culture, the way Idris steered it boldly into the future with a solid understanding of his nation's past. And knowing all of these things, owning them in her heart, gave her strength to lift her head up from her notes and begin to speak.

She found herself boldly looking directly into camera lenses, explaining the finer points of the gene therapy they hoped Amira would benefit from. When a reporter would ask her a question, instead of her insides being reduced to a wobbly jangle of nerves, she felt her spine straighten, and clear, concise answers come out of her mouth. At moments, it was almost as though she was looking at herself through the reporters' lenses, seeing a confident, intelligent, capable woman.

"And what of Her Highness?" one particularly insistent reporter asked. "How aware is the Sheikha of what will be happening to her?"

"Very much," Robyn answered. "I have explained the surgery and gene therapy to her—along with her father's input, of course—until I was confident she fully understood the process."

"Aren't you just setting her up for disappointment?" another jumped in.

"How do you mean?"

"If it doesn't work."

"That's always a possibility," Robyn replied, astonished she wasn't scooping up all of her paperwork and fleeing. Admitting something she was going to do could be a failure was not normally something she conceded to with confidence. But this time around, it felt as if part of her had been in hiding and had finally come out into the light for a grand reveal. All of the trust and confidence her colleagues had invested in her suddenly had merit. She knew where it had come from. The fire. The newfound strength.

It came from the enigmatic and utterly engaging Sheikh of Da'har. The dark-haired man sitting alongside her as she spoke, hands folded loosely on top of his knee, nodding, occasionally offering a supportive smile as he invested the most precious thing of all in her abilities: trust.

He was telling the world loud and clear he was trusting Robyn Kelly with his daughter's well-being and the swell of pride she felt in that knowledge was all she needed to make the press conference a success.

She leaned forward, eyes scanning from reporter to reporter, and spoke with a voice she hardly recognized as her own. "There are only a handful of hospitals in the world capable of such cutting-edge surgery. And of that handful, we at Paddington Children's Hospital are the only ones brave enough to do it."

"You mean *you're* the only one brave enough to do it?" shouted a reporter with a British accent.

Robyn shrugged. Wasn't that apparent? It was hardly her style to jump up and shout, "Yeah! I'm the best in the world!" She turned at the unexpected sound of Idris's voice.

"I think you'll find Dr. Kelly is in a league of her own. There is no one else to whom I would entrust my daughter's care. And just so we are clear—" Idris leaned forward, forearms pressed on the table, chin cocked to one side, the press mimicking the gesture as if magnetically drawn to him "—Her Royal Highness is living a rich and full life. This is not a win or lose situation. This is all gain." He shot Robyn a grateful look before continuing. "Dr. Kelly is the only surgeon I would trust to take on such a monumentally important surgery and Paddington Children's Hospital has the very best of facilities for the intricate surgery. Their long-established record of succeeding where other hospitals have not has earned my complete confidence. If, for whatever reason, her hearing is not restored, my daughter will continue to live a meaningful and well-balanced life—not least of which will include one day taking the reins of leadership in Da'har."

All eyes swung to Robyn. She surprised herself by meeting the gape-jawed looks with a confident smile. "Thank you very much for coming.

The next time we see you will be in London after what we expect will be a successful surgery."

She stood and gave a slight bow of the head as she'd seen many Da'harian women do when a conversation had finished. A quick glance over her shoulder as she turned to walk out of the auditorium told her Idris was close enough for her to hear his whispered words. "You dazzled them."

Lil' ol' plain Jane Robyn Kelly! Barren spinster. The woman who knew the nooks and crannies of Paddington's better than she did the cupboards of her own home. And now a media darling! It was one of those moments when all you could do was laugh at the madness of how far she'd come from thinking of herself as the barren spinster of Paddington's.

Getting to this point hadn't been a solo flight, though. It had been a duet.

"How would you feel about taking a walk with me?" Idris poked his head into Amira's room where she and Robyn had gone to read after supper. He'd looked in earlier and had barely been able to wipe the smile off his face for the last hour. Two heads—one blond, the other dark—pressed together as they worked their way through the intricacies of the elaborate tale. From what he could determine there were swashbucklers, princesses and a rather unfortunately named camel.

"Robyn?"

He took a step into the room, his smile grow-ing softer, more tender, as he took in the sight of the pair of them, fast asleep on Amira's large canopy bed. His daughter was curled in the crook of Robyn's arm, the book having spilled to one side. Robyn's body language was entirely open and loving, even in her sleep. Her cheek was resting atop of Amira's dark hair, one arm pro-tectively wrapped around his little girl's shoul-ders, the other enclosing Amira in a loose hug. Throughout Robyn's time in Da'har, there had, not even for a moment, been anything awkward or strained about the way the pair were with each other, and in sleep, the relationship they shared seemed, if possible, even more honest. One trust-ing soul with another.

He watched them for a moment before silently padding over to the bed and gently extracting Amira from Robyn's embrace so that he could tuck her under the covers. She stirred a little as he moved her, sleepily crooking the stuffed el-ephant she favored under her arm as he pulled up the covers and switched off the bedside lamp.

Walking around to the other side of the bed he wondered for a moment if he shouldn't just leave Robyn. She looked more relaxed and at peace than he had probably ever seen her. A swell of pride took hold of his chest as he remembered how well she had done at the press conference, despite her long-held fear of public speaking. Pride was replaced by passion as the desire to touch her, hold her in his arms, took such strong possession of him; he was lifting her up and out of the bed before common sense could prevail.

Robyn's arms slid naturally across his shoulders and chest, cinching together at the base of his neck as, still half-asleep, she nestled her curly blond head into his shoulder. The touch of her silky hair upon his cheek, intermingling with the wildflower meadow scents that swirled around her, threatened to undo him then and there.

Before he thought better of it, he tipped down his chin and kissed her.

Robyn wasn't sure if she was dreaming or if she was receiving a very real kiss. She clenched her eyes tight, not wanting whatever was happening to come to an end. Hits of understanding came to her.

Idris's scent. Cinnamon and hot sun mixed with pure alpha male.

His touch. Fingertips pressing possessively along her midriff, shifting with intent along the silken top she wore over a pair of body-hugging *sherwal* trousers. A cascade of goosepimples shivered along her spine as more details came to her.

His arms were around her. One around her back and the other under her knees, holding her as if she weighed nothing more than sunshine itself.

His lips, which she could feel hovering just above hers, were every bit as sensuous as she had imagined them to be. The touch of them so soft and evocative... Surely this had to be a dream.

Her eyes fluttered open, lashes brushing against his soft skin, before their gazes locked and an understanding passed between them. The desire was mutual and pressing, unchecked, against doors they both wanted to open.

Her lips parted. She felt the brush of his stubble against her skin as he took possession of her mouth again. Hungry, heated kisses seared her to her very core and all she could think was...more.

Idris's spicy scent intermingled with the sweet taste of his lips. It was impossible to hold in a whimper as he drew his lips away from hers and began to drop kisses along the length of her neck. Softly at first and then, as her senses shot to life at the speed of light, the pressure from his lips grew more urgent. As he reached her throat, and then her mouth, his tongue took advantage of the parting of her lips as a low moan escaped her throat. Lightning jags of response crashed through her, jettisoning her entire body onto another plane of touch alight with electricity.

"I want you."

She could barely believe she'd spoken the words, but they were the truest thing she could say. She did want him. Body and soul she ached for him in a way she hadn't known possible.

Idris accelerated his pace, taking the length of the never-ending corridor in long-legged strides, turning, unexpectedly, into his own suite of rooms, which she hadn't yet seen.

The blur of decor she glimpsed as he carried her toward his emperor-size bed was deeply male. Rich scarlets, the darkest of blues and the raw luster of mahogany melded together to craft the extraordinary sensation of masculine beauty. Something Idris's entire being exuded. Especially now as he laid her out on his bed, chest heaving with ragged breaths, not from exertion but desire.

If he had wanted her to beg she knew she would have.

Never before had anyone looked at her with such longing. She could see the flashes and glints of hunger in his eyes, as if a damn had burst within his psyche. More than anything, she wanted to satiate his every appetite.

Lush, wanton thoughts crowded out the woman Robyn had thought she once was as a sexual confidence she'd never experienced took hold of her. She pressed herself up to sitting, tipped her chin up so that she could meet Idris's black, sparking gaze and reached out to touch him below his waist where his desire for her was most evident.

He gasped at the contact, instantly pulling her up so that her legs encircled his waist, both hands cupping her buttocks as his lips crashed down on hers with a heated urgency she ached to return. Such was the depth of her need for him, slaking her hunger for Idris's kisses, his touch, would be nigh on impossible.

Idris unhooked Robyn's legs from around his waist, his arms bearing her entire weight just millimeters away from his own as if it would help check his body's primal urges to possess her. Whether she was light as a feather or he was channeling the strength of a Titan—all he knew was he was holding an angel in his arms. Amber eyes. A halo of blond curls. The softest skin he had ever touched.

He laid Robyn onto his bed, standing stock-still for just a moment as he drank in the sight of the wild, desire-fueled woman he'd uncaged. He lowered his knees to the edge of the bed, then fully mounted it, crawling slowly forward as a triumphant lion would approach a prospective mate, to take possession of what he knew he had already won.

The tight line of connection that had drawn them together cinched and became unbreakable.

Idris's lips peeled into a satisfied smile with each whimper and groan of pleasure he drew from her. The simplest of movements—a finger tracing the soft outline of her jaw, his lips skidding across the décolletage of her *dishdasha*, a thumb grazing the sides of her straining breasts as he lowered his mouth to kiss them through the thin fabric—each gesture elicited a complexity of responses.

There was much more than lust in those amber eyes of hers, and when she whispered into his ear, he could have sworn she told him that she would always be his. Only be his.

An even deeper longing for Robyn shunted straight to his heart, spreading like scintillating pulses through his entire bloodstream. Theirs was a mixture of primal and cerebral, an inevitable union as the stars aligned for them. For tonight, at least, they would be as one.

Robyn's body positively thrummed with need. She began, timidly at first, then insistently, to undo the buttons on Idris's shirt, then his trousers. His impatience matched hers and within milliseconds he had dispensed of his clothes and her own.

When the length of his naked body pressed against hers, a cry of longing so carnal she barely knew where it had come from curled up and out of her throat. Each of his touches was pure erotica. The caress of his hands. The sensation of his bedclothes against her skin as he moved her to where he could please her best. The soft hair on his leg as he wound it around hers, decreasing the ever-diminishing space between them. The wet warmth of his mouth traveling from her breasts to her belly and beyond—all threatened to be her undoing.

Her body became possessed by a need to touch and be touched, to have him inside her, deep and unfettered. After an agony of strokes and teases, Idris slipped a hand between her legs, fingers slowly sliding along the length of her wetness before pulling his hand along her inner thigh until he reached her knee, tugging her leg onto his back as he lowered himself into the hot, eager center of her very womanhood.

It was the first time in Robyn's life she had experienced complete, full-bodied ecstasy at the touch of another man. Her body melded with his as their movements intensified, each of them undulating and pressing together to reach the ultimate release, until finally, when she felt they could fly no higher, everything within her burst into a shimmering cloud of sensation and pleasure. Idris reached the same heated denouement deep within her, his spine arching, belly pressing into hers as Robyn's nails scored the length of his back, eliciting a whimper of the purest satisfaction from her parted lips.

They lay in silence, each of them taking long, full-bodied lungfuls of air as their bodies recovered. Idris shifted to his side, pulling Robyn in tight to him so that her back met his stomach and chest, the beat of his heart pumping straight through to her own. As their heartbeats synchronized and slowed, she knew, at long last, she would sleep without dreams, for everything she could have hoped for was right there next to her.

CHAPTER TEN

DAWN WAS ONLY just creeping into the room when Idris inhaled a deep breath of wildflowers and sunshine—the scent of heaven if ever there was one. It took a moment or two to realize he was still holding Robyn in his arms. If anything, she had nestled in closer in the course of the night; their limbs were softly tangled. Her soft curls tickled and teased the side of his cheek and life seemed near enough perfect until he realized, with a deafening pound of his heart, that Amira might come in at any moment. It happened more often than not. When she'd had a bad dream, or a question about a book she was reading.

Mouth dry, pulse racing, his mind thundered with possibility.

Would it be so bad if she were to find them?

He had ached for the fact his daughter had no mother figure. Someone to speak with about the myriad things only women share with one another. Someone to light up her somber world. Someone who would be there for her when, one day, Amira ascended into womanhood. He knew playing the roles of both mother and father only went so far, and yet… He was already asking her to trust in Robyn regarding the operation. If that were to fail…?

He extracted himself, as gently as possible, from the weave of their limbs, not wanting to wake her before he knew where he stood on… what exactly? It wasn't as if he and Robyn were going to have a life together! She lived in England—in Paddington's by all counts. He had a nation to rule, a daughter to raise—to the very best of his undivided attentions.

The decision to make love to Robyn suddenly seemed careless. Not a decision at all but an impulse. A matter of the heart he should have overruled with his conscience. Falling in love with Robyn—what could that lead to?

A jagged slash of pain rent through him so completely he could have sworn he'd been split in two. Physical proof he had nothing to offer her beyond a heart battered and singed by life's crueler turns.

Robyn. Beautiful, sunlit, optimistic Robyn, who had brought nothing but kindness and light into their lives.

He took another step back from the bed and began yanking on his trousers and then his shirt, as if they would shield him from the desire to crawl back into her arms and give himself over to the unknown.

His lips pressed and thinned against each other.

Robyn deserved more. And he had to slam shut the windows of opportunity that kept blinking at him. Hope. Possibility. Love.

He must lead, if he were to make good on the promises he'd made to the memory of his wife.

Everything for the past seven years had been solely for Amira and Da'har. Blood and country. It was how he'd survived. There hadn't been room in his heart for anything more.

He looked down at Robyn, her face soft with the innocence of sleep.

How reckless he'd been! Selfish even, to have pulled her so close to him when he didn't have a full and open heart to offer her. Robyn deserved every bit of a man's heart. *His heart.* But after all he'd been through, it was no longer his to give.

The thoughts whirling in his brain began to compound with viselike strength. How was he going to get out of this without hurting Robyn?

He shook his head knowing damn well how he would deal with it. Precisely the same way he'd made it through the tragedy that had blindsided him all those years ago. By steeling his heart and realigning his focus. Blood and country. Nothing more.

It didn't take Robyn long to figure out something was wrong. Her legs and arms were wriggling about in a luxurious stretch when, still half-asleep, she realized the sheets she was tugging up and over her shoulder were the ones in her own bedroom. She sat bolt upright, her heart stopping dead still, then unleashing in a series of staccato pumps. One for each question flying through her mind. How did she get here? Where was Idris? Had last night been a dream?

She threw back the covers and tugged on some clothes, barely noticing it was perfectly natural for her to reach for the formfitting leggings and loose tunic native to Da'har. All she could think of was whether or not she had done something wrong. Had she upset Idris in some way? Spoken in her sleep about—what? Paddington's?

She tried to push away the hurt she was feeling, certain there was some sort of simple explanation. It wasn't as if she'd been expecting rose petals, a perfect cup of Earl Grey and a plate of freshly baked scones to arrive on her lap, but after the night they'd shared she'd expected...*something*.

No. That wasn't right, either.

She'd expected *someone*.

Idris.

This was a message. It had to be. A cruel one. Depositing her back in her bed after— A shiver of response slipped along her spine at the memory of her night in Idris's arms. Only to be left on her bed as if it had meant nothing?

She sped along the corridor toward his office, little snippets of possibility taking form in her head, then reshaping over and over as she blindly made her way past the tiles, fountains and tumbles of lush vegetation that, until now, had never failed to enchant her.

Was he *ashamed* of what they had done?

Fear stole through her at the thought, chased cruelly by the anguish of loss. The same hollow feeling she hadn't experienced since her hysterectomy.

She'd been right two weeks ago. To want to stay in the UK. She'd told *everyone*! Coming to Da'har was ridiculous. She'd be out of her depth. Destroy any good that might come of doing Amira's operation.

Amira.

Paddington's.

The tight squeeze in her heart made her gasp. She'd let Idris's beautiful little girl slip too far into her heart, as well.

Idris.

A low moan escaped her lips as she thudded her forehead with the ball of her hand. How could she have let this happen when the only thing she should have been thinking of was saving Paddington's?

Idris had it all. Her heart, her body. What she had left of her mind was going to have to be put to exacting use, to regain what little control she had over her future. Over the future of Paddington's. If she had to fall on the sword of sacrifice, she would do it.

Her knuckles stung as she rapped on the carved wooden exterior of Idris's office. Too impatient to wait for a response, she pushed open the thick wooden door only to find a very officious-looking Idris sitting at his desk, pen in hand, a sheaf of papers laid out before him as if it were any old day.

Didn't he know her world had changed when she gave herself to him?

"Is that your luggage?" she asked inanely as a luggage-laden servant walked past from the room where they had spent the night wrapped in the other's arms.

"Yes," Idris replied, looking up from his paperwork as if her presence in his office was a complete mystery. Those dark eyes of his, so expressive the night before, were now impenetrable in their inky darkness. The glacial reserve she'd shivered under upon their first meeting was icily back in place. "It would probably be a good idea to get your things together. I can have someone else do it if you're busy. The plane will leave today at lunchtime."

"Plane?"

"Yes." He nodded as if she'd already been

given a rundown of the day's itinerary and hadn't burned it into her psyche as everyone else had. "To England."

"You're sending me back to England?"

His hardened features were a cruel confirmation of what she'd feared but never put words to. Her life would always be a lonely one.

"What about Paddington's?"

The question hung in the air between them until Idris pushed back from his desk with a harsh sigh he knew came across as exasperated when in fact he felt as if the universe was sucking his lungs dry. The look on Robyn's face told him everything he needed to know.

In one swift moment, he had torn each and every fiber of connection they'd shared in their short time together.

But it was the right decision. Whatever it was that had passed between them had to end. No amount of wide-eyed, bewildered amber looks would change his mind.

"We're *all* going to England. I've made the appropriate calls regarding Amira's admission into Paddington's and trust you are well placed to set the wheels in motion on your end. Sooner is better."

Robyn just stood and stared, her eyes swirling with confusion, appalled by his behavior.

He fought the urge to cross to her, hold her in his arms and tell her he knew he was being a fool. What would that do other than make things worse? The Idris he'd been over the past fortnight was gone now. The one who had felt happy. Contented. Prepared to face the world, at long last, with a smile. The shadow of a smile disappeared from his face. He couldn't be that man. Not with a daughter to raise. A kingdom to rule.

Robyn's unnatural silence threatened to be his undoing.

"I don't think I need to remind you, Dr. Kelly, that I have responsibilities that override your holiday plans being curtailed. Perhaps it's time to make good on all those promises you made at the press conference yesterday."

Her jaw dropped at his words.

"Dr. Kelly, we've not got much time and I'm quite busy. If you don't mind…" He gave his watch a cursory glance, ignoring the tangle of blond curls whose wisps had tickled along his cheek as they'd lain, limbs tangled together, in silken sheets. The amber eyes that had flickered with desire solely for him. The dusky rose lips that had whispered vows of commitment to him and him alone.

He slammed the door shut on the memories. He couldn't give her his lacerated heart. Not with the loss he'd suffered. Not with an empty palace standing in the center of the capital—a hollow testament to the love he had once had and could never have again. Not with Amira's future at stake.

He gritted his teeth and forced himself to swallow the bitter pill.

This had to end.

"Perhaps you could stop by Amira's room, suggest some things she might bring along for her stay in the hospital." His dismissive tone did not go unnoticed and, in true Robyn-style, he saw her heels press more soundly to the marble floor.

"Perhaps, as her *father*, you should explain to her what's going on."

"About what exactly, Dr. Kelly? She knew we'd be heading to London shortly."

Robyn staggered back a step, sending him a look of disbelief so powerful it pierced straight through to his soul.

He was handling this about as well as he had handled the loss of his wife—which was precisely the point. He wouldn't—*couldn't*—give Robyn his heart. And his priority was Amira. She was used to the harsher edges of his personality. Sharp contours that had softened with Robyn in their lives.

"Your Excellency," Robyn bit out, her voice now curling with well-deserved disdain, "while I appreciate your time is precious, it is my professional opinion that your priority right now is to be a father."

Idris swallowed the words as if they were poison.

"Are you suggesting my daughter is not my absolute priority?"

"Not at all. But I do know it can be difficult for a parent to put their child through an experimental operation like this. You want what's best for her, but it can be very frightening for both the patient and the parent."

She was giving him an out—an excuse for behaving abominably. One he couldn't take.

"I think you may have misread my intentions when I invited you to Da'har," Idris bit out, the words tasting acrid as they crossed his lips. "My daughter is my one, my only, focus. The flight will be leaving shortly. You'd be well advised to pack your things."

Robyn, to his astonishment, simply stood there, unblinking, her body soaking in the aftermath of his vile words. A jag of anger tore through him that she wasn't finding this as painful as he was. He willed the burning in his heart to turn to ice, barely recognizing his own voice when he finally broke the silence he'd forced upon them.

"Dr. Kelly, let's not add letting down Paddington's to the day's list of things to do."

He'd been certain she would cry. Flee the room.

Anything other than stand there and stare at him with her wide, amber eyes.

"You do remember you're human, don't you? That you're allowed to feel pain and fear, just like the rest of us mere mortals."

Robyn's voice was steady as she handed him the olive branch, a move far too generous for someone who'd received such an unkind verbal swipe. Where he had become cold-blooded, she had become brave. A modern-day Boadicea, fearlessly protecting all that she held to be true. If his daughter's welfare weren't at stake, he'd see his own behavior as cowardice. But he had her heart to defend as well as his own and this was the only way he knew how.

Robyn shook her curls away from her eyes and met Idris's gaze with an intensity she hardly knew she possessed. He may not love her, but she would not let him rob her of her dignity in the process.

"If you don't mind me saying, it's not right what you're doing. Living in the past isn't going to help your daughter."

"I most certainly do mind!" His hand slapped against the mahogany sheen of his desk with a resounding clap, making it clear Robyn was stepping into extremely unwelcome territory. "Amira *is* my way of looking forward."

"You're imposing responsibilities on a child that you should be carrying!" she shot back.

"And I suppose your rich and varied experience as a parent enables you to make all these wise decisions?"

Robyn looked away, her throat constricting against a swell of nausea. She knew Idris wasn't biting out at her. He was angry with the world, but whenever the barbs from a frightened parent became personal these were the moments that hurt the most. The judgments people made just because she didn't have children of her own. As if they thought being barren rendered her incapable of empathy, of love.

She closed her eyes for a moment, imagining she was back in one of the family rooms at Paddington's. White coat over sensible attire. Parents looking at her with wide-eyed disbelief that the perfect child they'd created was in hospital. A mixture of hope that whatever she said would fix it all and fear that life as they knew it would never be the same. All of the Pennys and Ryans flickered past her mind's eye and poured the strength she needed back into her heart.

"Idris, Your Excellency, I may not have a child of my own, but I have spent each and every day of my professional life with children and their parents during their darkest hours. I have fallen in love with more of them than I can count. I have grieved with their parents when we have lost them. I have cheered alongside many more when their child, with Paddington's help, overcame some of life's cruelest hurdles. So, yes. I think my experience affords me a certain level of expertise in understanding when a parent's wishes interfere with a child's needs."

"Is that what you think I'm doing? Interfering?" Idris rose from his desk with a surge of unchecked fury that made Robyn grateful for the expanse of desk standing solidly between them.

"No. I think you are loving your daughter to the best of your ability."

"And in your eyes—" his voice grew colder as he spoke "—my 'ability' to love my daughter falls short?"

Oh, you want me to insult you? Kick you while you're down? Tough.

"I think you are capable of much more than you give yourself credit for," Robyn replied, the painful sting of tears teasing at the back of her throat. He may not love her, but she'd be damned if she was going to let him wallow in self-pity. He had life, a daughter, a kingdom! She gave Idris a curt nod. "If you'll excuse me, I'd better get my things together."

When she closed the door behind her, it took

everything in her power not to race to her room and release the flood of tears for all that she had gained and lost when she had left the safety of Paddington's behind.

CHAPTER ELEVEN

EVEN THE ROAR of the jet's engines couldn't drown out Idris's thoughts.

Robyn hadn't so much as said a word to him since they'd left the palace. Not that he blamed her. If he could pull back the sand that had swept through the hourglass since this morning he would have. Whatever had passed between them, she didn't deserve the icy blows he delivered with too much ease.

Seven years. Seven years of lashing out at a world that had done nothing but try and make up for the grief he couldn't bear to set aside.

He accepted a glass of sparkling water from the flight attendant, grateful for the fleeting diversion from his thoughts.

Amira, he noticed, was back to her sober little self. The ready smile she'd worn so often over the past week, the laughter, all hidden away.

His lips carved a scowl into the sides of his mouth, knowing they could be smiling and laughing right now if history hadn't ripped his heart out of his chest for daring to love. Trusting that such a perfect happiness would last.

Amira slipped out of the seat beside him, having teased the last of the stories out of him hours earlier. He reached out a hand to touch the long, slick gloss of hair, just missing the connection as she crawled into Robyn's lap. He watched, transfixed, as after a moment's discussion Robyn began to sing to her. His daughter's small fingers traced Robyn's lips as she mouthed along with her, occasionally forming words out loud, and in a bittersweet moment of perfection that nearly brought tears to his eyes, the pair hit a perfect harmony when their voices converged as one.

A flash of insight struck him. How talkative Amira had become since Robyn had been with them. Amira's voice bore the telltale thickness of a deaf child's, instinct unable to conquer the inability to hear, and yet, hearing her join in as Robyn sang about mockingbirds and diamond rings, he wondered how it would sound in a week's time, when Amira could hear her own voice.

Hot, searing pain rammed into his chest as he reminded himself Robyn would play little to no part of Amira's voyage of discovery. He'd made sure of that this morning.

"There, can you see?" Robyn stopped singing and pointed, then signed rapidly as she spoke to Amira. "London."

They each peered out of an oval window, Amira's face alight with interest as Robyn pointed out Buckingham Palace and the London Eye. Even Paddington's signature turrets were easy to spot from the flight path their pilot had taken. It was the place where his daughter's life would be changed forever—where both of their lives had already been changed by this whirlwind of a woman who had burst into his hotel room only a few weeks before.

He shifted in his seat, uncomfortable with the pendulum swing of his thoughts. He'd made his decision.

Even with only ten minutes to go, Robyn would have happily forsaken the luxury of his private jet for a knee-cramping, elbow-jabbing economy seat on an overcrowded commuter plane in lieu of enduring the torture of sitting across from Idris.

His eyes lifted to meet hers, the darkness of his irises, as ever, fathomless and inaccessible.

Her hands curled into fists, gathering up the thick fabric of the skirt she'd worn on the flight out. A pathetic gesture, really. As if her slim fingers could defend her from the churning disappointment and loss she knew she'd finally give in to when this was all over. Already she missed the silken caresses of the clothes she'd worn in Da'har. The exotic, hot scents of the country. Idris's smile.

She sat back in the soft leather seat with a huff. Just thinking of pawing through her bag, finding her key, putting it in the lock of the flat she knew had never been a home, exhausted her. She'd probably slept more nights in the hospital's on-call rooms than at her "nest." It was neither nest, nor home. Just a place she hung her clothes in between surgeries.

Idris's palace in Da'har had been more of a home to her in less than a fortnight than her own had ever been.

Squeezing her eyes shut tight against the thought only let the darkness creep further into her overanxious heart.

She eased one eye open, then the other, blinkering her vision so that she could only see Amira. Her beautiful heart-shaped face. The sheet of ebony hair cascading down her slim, little shoulders. Robyn's chest squeezed tight when she saw the hope and light that lit up Amira's almond-shaped eyes when she realized Robyn was looking at her. Saying goodbye to this little girl was going to be particularly painful.

Swallowing down the tears she refused to let come, she pasted on a smile.

Never mind. She was back in London now. She could jump into a taxi and go straight to Paddington's where everything would right itself back into its natural order once again. What had happened in Da'har was…an aberration. A mirage more like, she silently chided herself. A beautiful, sand and sea and Idris-filled mirage.

She tugged a few folders out of her satchel, blindly training her eyes upon the papers as if the words she could barely focus upon would save her life.

The diagrams and side notes began to pull her back to her comfort zone and at long last she felt a smile begin to creep onto her lips. The surgery wouldn't save a life—but it would most assuredly change Amira's for the better.

As the plane touched down and she turned on her mobile, it sprang to life with some sobering news.

Ryan Walker had had a turn for the worse. The sooner she could get back to Paddington's and help with the fallout, the better. Ryan's brain injury wasn't her area of expertise, but the young boy had had the entire staff rooting for his recovery. Losing him now, when he'd fought so hard against the odds…

What was it Idris was fond of saying in his darker moments?

Life wasn't fair.

She pulled her satchel up onto her lap and unbuckled herself from the luxurious leather seat before giving Idris a quick nod. "I'll see you two tomorrow at Paddington's."

She planted a swift kiss on the top of Amira's head, and the moment the stairs were lowered to the private entrance, she began to run. Lungs burning, feet racing, heart pounding so hard she could hear nothing but the rush of blood in her head. She ran and ran until she was safely in a taxi heading back to Paddington's where she belonged.

The platter of chocolate-covered ginger biscuits stared at Idris accusingly. One side amber, the other inky black. He had half a mind to fling them off the balcony.

"Who on earth requested these?"

"No one. I think they just assumed, given your order from the last time we stayed, you might want them again?" Kaisha answered from under the desk where she had been plugging in the various laptops, mobiles and other electronics they never seemed to be able to travel without these days.

"I don't think we'll stay here next time," he growled. "If there is a next time."

"The hospital has offered you a suite at Paddington's if you prefer. Amira will need to be prepped and ready quite early tomorrow morning, so…" Kaisha crawled out from the desk, managing to intersect him as he stalked from room to room in the hotel suite he wished he'd never taken. It was too awash with memories of his first meeting with Robyn.

Across the suite, Amira's little face was pressed up against the rain-streaked windows as she stared at the iconic buildings they'd seen from the airplane. She was missing Robyn, too—and no amount of sterling British architecture would fill that gap.

Kaisha discreetly cleared her throat as she waited for an answer, only to stumble back a few steps as he wheeled on her, hands splayed out in disbelief.

"They think I'm going to be able to *relax* while my daughter's future is hanging in the balance?" Idris's eyes shot heavenward, realizing as he spoke that this could be the last time he could speak loudly, harshly even, without causing distress to his daughter, whose eyes were still glued to the London cityscape beyond the floor-to-ceiling windows.

He glanced at Kaisha, now slowly backing away from him, a hint of fear all too visible in her eyes. The same look she'd often worn before Robyn had come into their lives.

A streak of remorse twisted his features as he pressed his hands to his face. Had he used Amira's deafness as a means of justifying this way of speaking with people?

"I think it was more so you'd have somewhere private to—"

"To what?" Idris interjected. "Wait and find out if my daughter is still deaf?"

"I believe Robyn—Dr. Kelly, I mean..." Kaisha's voice faded out as the expression on Idris's face grew dark again.

Robyn. The light to his shade. The woman with courage enough to challenge him with what he himself could not bear to confront: his fear. The creeping, terrifying tendrils of laser-sharp fear threatening to drown him in darkness as the moment approached when he would hand over his daughter's welfare to—

The only woman in the world he would trust with her care.

He began to shake his head, eyes searching the growing darkness as night fell over London's skyline.

What had he done? How big a fool had he been?

"Anyone want to run through things one more time?"

Robyn held up her gloved hands and scanned the pairs of eyes peeking out at her from above their surgical masks. Sure they were only practicing on a model, but it was important to mimic the exact conditions in which they would be doing the operation.

Not a single headshake.

Just as it should be.

"May I get the case for the middle ear pieces, please, Rosie?"

"You got it, Robyn."

The flame-haired nurse carried over the special box that would house the miniscule middle ear replacement.

A rap on the door turned all of their heads.

"All right, Leo?" Robyn called out cheerily. "Ready to help out with prep tomorrow?"

The pediatrician stuck his head through the door with a smile. "Absolutely. Can't wait to be part of history in the making!"

He received a chorus of whoops in response. These were the moments when Paddington's really shone. They were an unbreakable team—particularly in the face of the unknown.

"Rosie, I'm heading down to the Frog and Peach. Meet me there?"

"Mmm?" Rosie stood absolutely still as Robyn loaded the precious pieces into the case, releasing an audible sigh as she did. "Sorry, love. I'll be there in half an hour."

"Va bene." Leo gave the door frame a clap and turned to go. "Get your beauty sleep, everyone. And best of luck!"

A chorus of thank-yous went up as the doctors and nurses meticulously returned their equipment to the exact location they would be expecting it in the morning.

"That was nice of Leo to pop in." Robyn pulled down her surgical mask and smiled, hoping the heat in her cheeks didn't betray the slightest—okay, the huge—bit of envy that Rosie had found love.

"I'd love to take all the credit." Rosie laughed. "But I think Leo's more interested in your surgery than me today. The whole hospital is on tenterhooks about tomorrow."

"What a relaxing thought!" Robyn's cheeks flared further. She didn't mind having an audience when she was in surgery, but knowing the future of the hospital was hanging in the balance because of this one, very risky surgery…

It was a lot of pressure she didn't need on top of a deflated heart and ego and the splattered remains of her pride. Maybe she could fling herself on the operating table after Amira's surgery and demand returning cardiologist, Dr. Wolfe, throw a few well-placed stitches into her broken heart.

She smiled at the image her mind's eye conjured and shook her head. See? Losing the man she'd never had wasn't hurting that badly, after all. She was already able to make jokes about it—albeit to herself—but it was precisely the sort of thing she hoped would happen when she'd walked back through the high Victorian arches of Paddington's.

"Why don't we call it a day, then?" Robyn tugged her mask free of her neck, giving the collection of esteemed surgeons and specialists the best smile she could muster. "We'll all need to be here bright and early."

She loitered while they made their way out in twos and threes, some making dinner plans, others announcing their intention to have an early night after grabbing a quick drink at the Frog and Peach. An urge to go with them to the "hospital pub" overtook her. She could have a glass of soda water and lime—her go-to favorite when she wasn't in the mood for an alcoholic drink. Just a chance to relax before heading to her home-not-home. Or not…

The double doors to the surgical theater *phwapped* shut and, at long last, she was alone. She stared at the model they'd been working on, superimposing Amira's little face onto the silicone one in front of her, only just stopping herself from reaching out and stroking the long, ebony hair that wasn't there.

Amira's hair would have to be partially shaved. Just a little bit behind and above her ears. Her bright eyes would be closed, her head tipped to the side so they would have full access to her ear.

She'd have a scar—a small one tucked behind her ear—but the surgery would mark her no matter what the result. It would be the first step in a long road, including speech therapy, follow-up gene therapy and some six months' worth of checkups before she should receive maximum hearing. In other words—this was the beginning of a difficult journey for Amira. Maybe she would get her a service dog to see her through the transition. A beautiful hearing dog. The three of them could—

Robyn gasped, unable to stem a sob as reality reared upon her like a wild stallion.

The three of them could nothing. They weren't a threesome. There was no "we" or "us."

The only thing she could do was perform a flawless operation.

No pub. And she wouldn't bother with going home. Twiddling her thumbs on her own would only drive her mad.

Maybe she'd relieve Ryan's parents from the vigil they were holding by his bedside. Poor little chap. He'd been through so much and to fall into a coma at this point? His parents had looked wrecked when she'd stopped in to chat with them. A nap in the family room was probably overdue. She'd offer to read to him.

Her brain scanned through the vast book collection in her office. A fairy tale? Nothing too gruesome, though. She bit down hard on her lip a little too aware she'd need a huge injection of courage, as well.

This was her forte. Her strength. Medicine had always been her right-hand man and she wouldn't be trying the surgery if she didn't have complete and utter confidence in her success.

Then, for once in her life, maybe the planets would align and Paddington's would be saved and she'd never have to think about the man who'd stolen her heart ever again. Perhaps tomorrow she could arrange a nice little case of amnesia…

She laughed and pushed out of the empty lab to go check on the three-dimensional printer, still hard at work making a backup set of the middle ear pieces.

Malleus. Incus. Stapes.

Each tiny, perfectly shaped piece would play a vital role in Amira's ear.

A trill of excitement took spark and held, lighting her smile properly for the first time since she'd returned. Leaving Idris and Amira so brusquely had felt like ripping off one of her own limbs. When the surgery was done and dusted tomorrow, maybe she'd feel whole again.

CHAPTER TWELVE

THE CLOCK HAND dropped a single measly stop. Two hours and forty-three minutes since Amira had been taken into surgery. Each painful second after the last, moments ticking away with the exhaustive slowness of sap running from a tree, drip by even slower drip with no concern for those who lay in wait.

Idris forced himself to sit down in the softly lit "family room." There'd be holes in the practical, overdesigned carpet if he didn't cool his jets.

A low growl formed and flew out of his throat unchecked. He was beginning to wish he'd taken the hospital up on its offer of a suite. Not for the luxury of it, but for the rooftop space. He could pace freely there. Shake his fist skyward. Even the illusion of being able to roar from the rooftops if things didn't go as planned would provide some release to the agony he was feeling.

He thought of Robyn's beautiful face and knew he'd find solace there whatever the outcome.

Solace he didn't deserve.

Those amber eyes of hers, ever generous even though he'd been unnecessarily cruel.

This morning, when she'd entered Amira's room to bring her up to the surgical ward, she'd managed a smile. Some kind words. Her touch, when she'd reached out to put her hand upon his wrist, had been a salve against the strains of the day.

"We'll do our very best."

Those were the final words she'd spoken to him and he believed her. Heart and soul he believed her. Which was a damn lucky thing because the feeling of sheer helplessness encapsulating him now was suffocating.

Every fear that could have come his way was piercing him in psychic knife blows so vivid he was surprised the waiting room wasn't running with blood.

Had he pushed Amira into this?

Was the risk worth it?

An abrupt shift change crowded all his other thoughts away.

It wasn't the risk of surgery he was worried about. How *blind* he'd been. All his anger, the crudely executed rage—it was all cruel bluster to mask the truth that lay within his heart.

He loved Robyn.

Loved her with every fiber of his being. Not to act on that love would be to condemn himself and his daughter to a lifetime of fear and pain that neither of them deserved.

He closed his eyes, fingers spread wide on the sofa cushions as he pictured the woman he'd married nine years earlier. Her beautiful smile, the soft laugh and almond-shaped eyes he saw every time he looked at their daughter.

A warm heat filled his chest as he thanked her for the love they had shared and the daughter she had bravely borne him at the cost of her own life. The heat strengthened and grew within him as he asked for her blessing to leave the days of mourning in his wake and fill them instead with a life of love and laughter only a future with Robyn could bring.

When at long last he opened his eyes, he knew there was only one thing he could do.

"All right, everyone, are we ready for the stapedotomy stage?"

Robyn took the familiar scan, cataloging the nods and yeses. "Okay, let's get that eardrum elevated and turned."

This was where she was in her element. Where she felt her confidence was best placed. Time became irrelevant. Energy continued unabated. All that mattered was the patient.

Through the operating microscope she watched her instruments as her hands elevated and turned the miniscule eardrum forward.

Robyn's concentration intensified, each movement more critical than the last.

The laser to vaporize select parts of the middle ear. The placement of a platinum piston. Connecting the piston to the second hearing bone—now the 3-D printed incus they had inserted earlier was in place.

Each step required follow-on steps, all of which would take months to be fully realized. But once they had injected the engineered virus designed to encode the ear's crucial microvilli, Amira should, pending the level of swelling, be able to tell them if the operation had been successful.

A cloth was passed across Robyn's brow. She glanced up from the surgical spectacles and saw the clock. Four hours. Only a few more steps to go—none of them rushed—and Idris could see his daughter again. She closed the mental door on what would follow. The only thing she could think about right now was Amira and the chance the little girl might have to hear.

"How long will it take?" His voice was low, but impatience snapped and crackled in Idris's every word. His body was taut with a barely contained frustration. An energy so charged Robyn could easily envision it coiled like a whip ready to lash out in biting snaps and flares at anyone or anything that stood in the way of his daughter's recovery.

She kept her eyes glued on Amira. It was the only way to keep her emotions in check. Of course, she couldn't blame Idris for being anxious, tense even, but he wasn't the only one clock-watching.

"It can take between ten and twenty minutes from now."

"That long?"

The strain had turned his voice hoarse. His tapping fingers drummed out all of the unspoken words on the doorframe.

I've already waited five hours and now you want more of my precious time?

"I'm not sure if you remember," Robyn began cautiously, "but Amira seemed to really enjoy the folk music we heard back in Da'har."

"You think I would've forgotten something like that?" Idris's dark-eyed gaze snapped to her, demanding her attention. She inhaled a deep breath, held it and looked up, almost frightened to see the emptiness in those jet-black eyes she had fallen in love with.

When her eyes met with his, she was physically struck by the story they told. Of course he remembered that day in the tent. They had laughed, sung and danced as a *family* that day. It was one of the pivotal moments, she was certain of it, that had led to their beautiful night back at the palace.

"Well, anyway—" she looked away, unable to bear the memories "—I hope you don't mind but I downloaded some music and thought I might put it on so Amira could wake to it."

"How on earth did you find Da'harian folk music?"

His bewilderment gave him a slightly more human edge, one that softened the sharp lines and angles of the man who held her heart in captivity.

A smile tweaked at the edges of her lips despite the rivulets of anxiety weaving their way through her nervous system. "I had a lot of… extra energy last night. I thought it best if I put it to some use."

"Trawling the internet for arcane folk music?"

"If by arcane you mean beautiful—" she shot back only just stopping herself from launching into a full speech telling him what she well and truly thought of him, how he was behaving, how ridiculous it was to be so miserable when all they had to do was open their hearts to love.

Or something like that.

"I'm trying," Idris ground out, "to *thank* you."

"Well, you might need to work on your delivery," Robyn parried with a huff that collapsed into a sigh. No matter what happened today, her journey with Amira and Idris was over.

Best to retain what few shreds of dignity the situation could afford her. She shifted on the bouncy rubber of her favorite trainers and wished, for the moment, she hadn't worn the smiley-face surgical cap she was only just remembering to take off. Looking goofy while your heart was breaking really was an unneeded lavishing of icing on the misery cake.

"Perhaps, Dr. Kelly, it might be a good idea to play the music."

Both of them stood tall, heels ground solidly into the hard hospital floor, eyes locked and trying to divine if they were fighting or agreeing.

Amira's small body lay between them, her hands resting atop the multicolored coverlet Idris had insisted they use in lieu of the regulation-issue sheets and blanket, her breath coming steady and slow. Robyn ached to touch her, stroke her soft little cheek, cup it with her hand. Kiss her darling sweet brow, tucking a few strands of silky hair back behind her ear, but knowing she couldn't now that Idris was here. Amira wasn't hers to love, but love her she did. With every aching pore in her body. Every bit as much as she loved the girl's stubborn, beautiful, irritating-in-ways-she-hadn't-imagined-possible father. The one whose eyes she could feel burning into her the longer she refused to obey.

Amira shifted ever so slightly. The last thing in the world Robyn wanted was for Amira to wake up and find two scowls hovering above her. Amira, on this day more than most, needed to wake up and see love. Because of her, for her, Robyn dug a hand into her white coat and pulled out her phone, fingers flashing along the touchscreen to find the music that had played throughout the entire surgery, fueling her to do her best.

Idris watched as Robyn, cheeks flushed with emotion, plugged the phone's attachment unit into the speaker and pressed Play.

"It might be a good idea if you sat alongside her, maybe held her hand." Her amber eyes lifted to meet his, then fluttered away just as quickly.

"Should I be facing her, or holding her?"

"Face her," Robyn gently encouraged. "If the surgery went as well as we believe, she should be able to hear you, but her brain will take some time to catch up with everything she is experiencing so you may want to sign, as well. She's used to reading your lips, so just behave as you always have with her."

Idris nodded, his chest constricting with emotion. This would be the first time his little girl would hear him speak. Robyn's calming instructions were the only things keeping him afloat as his mind raced with things to say.

Why hadn't he thought of this before? Would the simplest but truest of sentiments be the best? *I love you.* Or should it be a prayer of thanks? The name of their country. How much would compute with the words she read upon his lips with the sounds she would be hearing for the very first time?

Hello? Or perhaps, *Can you hear me?* So basic, but straight to the point. He cut himself short when he realized he was about to swear with frustration. He certainly wasn't going to have that be the first thing his cherished daughter heard!

The importance of language had never stood out so vividly before. His daughter would be *hearing* him. He clenched his eyes tight and tilted his chin up to the invisible heavens offering prayer upon prayer that the operation had been a success.

Idris tucked his fingers beneath Amira's hand when she stirred again. As her fingers clenched and released upon his own, Idris's blood began to rush and flow with the urgency of a river in a spring thaw. He forced himself to take slow, steadying breaths, not wanting to miss a single moment of his daughter's experience. This was for her. Everything was for her. Having Robyn here with them—the very reason this miracle might occur—was the most natural thing in the world. Without her…

He forced himself to align his scattered thoughts with the music, humming distractedly at first, then with a greater depth of feeling as he realized the reason the tune was striking such an emotional chord deep within him was because it was the very same song he had sung to Amira on that glorious day in the desert. The words came back to him, fitfully at first, and before he knew it, he was singing to his daughter. It was an ever hopeful serenade that would mark the success or failure of the incredible risk they had just taken.

Midway through the now familiar chorus, her small fingers squeezed his. Amira's eyes were still shut tight, but her forehead was crinkling in a show of confusion at first, then suddenly her eyes shot wide open, so quickly Idris forgot to keep singing.

"Keep singing, keep singing," Robyn encouraged, tears forming in her eyes as she took Amira's other hand.

Amira turned to her as she spoke and it was at that moment Idris understood that the surgery had been a success. Tears he'd never spilled flooded his eyes, blurring the beautiful expression on his daughter's face as she took in the same information he was processing.

She could hear.

Robyn had done exactly what she had promised. She'd made his daughter's near impossible dream a reality.

"Would you like to try talking?" Robyn asked Amira.

The little girl nodded, her features crumpling into sobs of understanding at the enormity of the moment. Idris, unable to bear even the tiniest sliver of fear his daughter might experience, forced himself to sing again, his voice so gruff with emotion, but it didn't matter. Not if it would help Amira take the first of many scary steps as she adjusted to the panoply of changes she would experience over the coming months. When his voice cracked, or faltered, Robyn joined in, her soft alto ribboning around his, giving him the strength and confidence to be the man he needed to be in this moment.

Amira's lips parted, her dark almond-sloped eyes shifting in wonderment between the pair of them, now singing like a couple of giggling teens.

"I can hear you," she finally said, tears pouring down her cheeks. "I can hear the song I felt you sing!" She pressed her hands to each of their chests in utter amazement that one beautiful thing had transformed into the other—into sound!

Her head whirled around, eyes narrowing as she sought the source of the other noises in the room. She played the air drums for a minute and signed to Robyn she didn't understand.

"It's music. You're hearing music coming from the speaker."

Amira's lips shaped into an astonished O as she looked at the small phone in disbelief.

"It's just how I imagined it! Beautiful!" she signed, then again and again made the beautiful swooping sign that meant *music*, shifting her fingers into the little bird that symbolized Robyn's name.

"Thank you," she said, turning her full attention to Robyn. "Thank you."

"I am so happy for you," Robyn signed back, her voice catching with emotion. "You deserve all the joy you receive in your new life."

"I'm so happy for all of us!" Amira shouted, then winced at the volume of her voice. "Have I always been this loud?" she whispered sheepishly.

Their collective laughter swirled up and around them, and before Idris could get his head around the fact his daughter had heard his voice for the very first time, she was clambering out from under the covers and tugging him and Robyn into a tight hug as she sobbed and sobbed with disbelief and joy.

As soon as she could bear to break herself away, Robyn excused herself.

She stood at the doorway, watching father and

daughter grasp and explore the new world Amira was beginning to inhabit, then turned and fled knowing the happy tears she had shed would now be weighted with sorrow.

"He wants to what?" Robyn had only just managed to splash water on her face, mortified her blotchy, tear-streaked face was going to have to appear on television! "No. Absolutely not. He can do it on his own. Amira is his daughter. This is their moment."

"That's not what he thinks, Robyn." Victoria fixed her with a friendly glare if ever such a thing were possible.

"Who? Dominic?" Robyn's face screwed up in a show of confusion. "Is he putting you up to this?"

"No, silly. Idris Al Khalil—you know, the multi*billionaire* Sheikh of Da'har—thinks so. He chose you out of dozens of possible surgeons to operate on his daughter. You've done what no one else in the world has managed and now you don't want him to sing your praises to the world?"

"Not on television, I don't." *Not anywhere.* It would be too much to bear. She didn't want to hear kind words when the paths their lives were taking would now split and veer off in very different directions.

"Stop being ridiculous. They've already set up

a press podium outside the hospital. Half the staff are out there already."

"What?" Robyn recoiled from the friendly hand her friend was rubbing along her arm. "In front of all the Castle's supporters *and* the press? Have you gone absolutely stark-raving *mad*? No, no, no, no, no." Her jaw clamped shut as she rigorously shook her head. Absolutely not. Humiliation one-on-one with Idris was one thing. But in front of all those people?

"Do I need to repeat the *billionaire* part or the *groundbreaking surgery* part?" Rosie intoned.

"I never agreed to do this for the money," Robyn grumbled. She'd never known she would lose her heart, either, but that hadn't stopped her from performing the surgery. Or from a whirlwind of heartbreak picking her up and swirling her around and around in the wake of Idris's rejection. She'd done too much acquiescing to His Excellency as it was. His Glowering Grumpency was more like it.

"Are you going to let a few jitters keep Paddington's from getting the well-deserved publicity your surgery could garner?" Victoria could scarcely keep the disbelief from her voice and Robyn didn't blame her. It was why she'd chosen her to front the campaign. She embodied everything Robyn didn't—confidence, the ability to have a baby, fall in love…

Ugh! Anger, anger, anger.

She didn't do anger, but it seemed to work for Idris—so it was going to have to work for her.

"Robyn." Victoria plopped her hands on each of her friend's shoulders. "You can do this. It'll be five minutes in and out and then you can hide away in the operating theater for the rest of your life if you please. Five. Minutes."

Robyn nodded, a sheepish smile creeping onto her face despite herself. "All right, you win!" She rocked back on her heels, tugged a tissue out of a nearby box and gave Victoria an impressed smile. "Dominic didn't stand a chance with you, did he?"

Victoria, to her credit, flushed with pride, her hands gliding across the ever-increasing swell in her belly. A baby, a fiancé—the paramedic's life seemed fairy-tale perfect after the storms she'd weathered. Robyn was seized by an impulse and pulled her into a hug. "Thanks for everything. You and Dom have done an amazing job handling the Save Paddington's campaign."

"Are you—" Victoria began, her voice muffled in Robyn's shoulder, then pulled back, her lips pressing into a frown as she inspected her tearstained face. "You didn't have a disagreement with the Sheikh or anything, did you?"

"Idris? No!" Robyn protested, throwing in a hand-wave, as if the gesture would punctuate the message she was trying and failing to get across. She was cool. Everything was *fine*.

She muffled a little sobby hiccup behind a fistful of tissues.

Victoria shot her a look, making it clear Robyn was going to have to work on her fake happy face. But it was the only face she had and all it could do was tell the truth. Her heart was no longer safely tucked away. She'd taken it out to play and had lost the game.

She gave her shoulders a little shruggy shake. "C'mon. Hanging out here isn't doing Paddington's any good. Let's give Idris his press conference and then I could do with a nice glass of wine over at the Frog and Peach if you're willing!"

"It's soda water for me," Victoria gently reminded her, an apologetic wince scrunching her features together when Robyn's eyes flooded with tears. "Maybe we could go somewhere else. Somewhere less...doctory?"

Robyn nodded, knowing if she spoke it would all come out. Her battered and bruised heart that had opened and fallen in love, not just with Idris but with Amira. The gut-wrenching pain at having to say goodbye after feeling, for the very first time in her life, like she was part of a family of her own.

"C'mon. Hand over your makeup bag. Let's

get you all freshened up so you can dazzle the masses!"

She let Victoria riffle through her small makeup bag. Powder, a bit of blusher and a fresh swipe of mascara improved things a little bit. They both turned and stared at her reflection. Back to cheery-faced Robyn!

At least on the outside.

"Ready for a bit of stiff upper lip and a smile for the cameras?" Victoria asked.

"As I'll ever be!"

The speed with which the press had gathered made Idris wonder if they'd been here all along. Awaiting the outcome of his daughter's surgery as anxiously as he had.

Good.

All the better. Paddington's deserved all the publicity in the world for their achievements today. For Robyn's achievements.

He turned to face the crowd with renewed vigor.

"The diligent care Dr. Robyn Kelly gave my little girl was above and beyond the treatment any parent would expect for their child."

Idris caught Robyn's eye for just a moment and took heart from her soft, beautiful smile. He hoped she knew he was speaking from the heart and not just trotting out niceties for the sake of a few moments on television. "I think Dr. Kelly knows me well enough by now," he continued, his voice suddenly constricting with a depth of emotion he never displayed in public, "to understand how very much giving the gift of hearing to my daughter meant not only to me but to her. As the future leader of Da'har—" He stopped, forced himself to blow out a steadying breath. "As the future leader of Da'har, my daughter's keenest wish was to be able to hear the voices of the people she would one day lead. In speech..." He turned to Robyn, knowing the only approval he needed was from the woman right next to him. "And in song. Today, not through a miracle of modern medicine but through the sheer determination, intelligence and unparalleled skills of Dr. Kelly and her team, Amira heard her father's voice join with her own in song." He choked back a sob and sucked in a deep breath before plunging forward. "Which is why I would like to announce my intention to make a donation to Paddington Children's Hospital, which should enable them to stay right here in the heart of London where they belong."

Robyn's eyes widened, only just containing a surge of tears.

The instinct to pull her into his arms told Idris everything he needed to know. History was just that. Now was the moment he needed to turn his full attention on the future.

"What surprised me the most along this journey we have taken with Dr. Kelly… Robyn…" He turned to her, stepping away from the podium, and reached out a hand. Reluctantly, her eyes darting to the crowd and the cameras, Robyn extended her hand to meet his. Electric shock waves crackled through him, assuring him he'd chosen to do the right thing.

"Robyn, you have not only restored my daughter's hearing, but you have restored my belief in love."

Conflicting emotions slammed into one another as Robyn tried to process what Idris was saying.

The rush of blood roaring between her ears all but drowned out her ability to hear him and she nearly laughed at the irony of it all—wishing he was signing as he spoke. She forced herself to focus on his lips—that beautiful mouth she had once kissed so passionately. She blinked as she saw his lips shape and form four words, then press together, an expectant, hopeful look lighting up those dark eyes of his. The hundred or so people watching the press conference gave a collective gasp as cameras whirred and clicked like mad.

"I'm sorry." Her fingers flew to her lips, not

entirely sure she'd heard him correctly. "Would you mind repeating that?"

She flushed as a wave of laughter rippled across the crowd, swirling and circling around her, proving, once again, that she absolutely did not belong in the limelight.

Idris smiled warmly, lovingly, stroking a hand across the back of Robyn's shaky palm.

"I asked you, my love, if you would do me the honor of marrying me." Idris smiled up at her, looking every bit the ardent lover he had been on that one precious night they had shared. Everything fuzzed and blurred around him. Was he… did he love her?

Scrunching her eyes together tightly, she popped them open again to make sure this wasn't a dream.

"But I thought…" She clamped her lips tight, not wanting the world's press to know they'd shared such an amazing night together that had ended in a humiliating rejection. He didn't want her. He'd made that clear. Hadn't he?

"I've learned so much in our time together," Idris said, his voice so quiet she had to strain to hear him. "Today I saw a future you were not a part of and I couldn't bear what I saw."

He rose, her amber eyes traveling along with his until her chin was tipped up, gazing into his face, seeking answers to myriad questions jockeying for pole position.

"You, Robyn Kelly, more than anyone I have ever met, have taught me the power of love. My country, my daughter and I all need you. We need your light, your laughter, the joy you bring to any situation. Your song is my song. Amira's song. Please say you will be my wife. A mother to Amira." He pressed a tender kiss upon the back of her hand and looked into her eyes, which had more light in them than ever before. "Let's become a family."

"A family?" Robyn repeated the words in a daze. "With you?"

Idris threw his head back and laughed. "Yes, with me! I'll gladly duel anyone who tries to step in and steal my woman." His voice softened again. "If you'll have me."

Robyn's head began to nod in infinitesimal little yeses. They gathered speed until she was nodding and shaking her head, tears springing to her eyes and scattering upon her cheeks.

"Yes!" she finally managed through the joy coursing through her every fiber. *A family.* "Yes."

Six months later

"I think you should be the one to cut the ribbon, Idris." Robyn decisively handed the ceremonial scissors back to her new husband. "You designed all of the changes."

"And you made all of the important suggestions!" he persisted, refusing to accept the silver-plated shears.

"I have a better idea," Robyn said, her smile growing as the possibilities it unleashed took flight. "Let's have Amira do it."

"Open the center?"

"Absolutely!" The idea grew and shone even brighter the more she thought about it. "Come." She grabbed ahold of his hand and took him back a few steps before turning to look at the former palace—once so cold and empty—now virtually abuzz with activity. "Look at what you've created. The Persian Gulf Language Center for the Deaf and Hard of Hearing. It will be amazing."

"You're the one who's amazing," Idris play-growled, nestling into the crook of his wife's neck, enjoying the tickly tease of her blond curls on his face as he did.

"*We're* amazing," she agreed with a big grin, wrapping her arms around his waist and giving him a kiss on his caramel-smooth cheek. "I never knew how much strength came from being a family. Thank you."

Idris laughed again. "We could go on like this all day, but we've got a center to open! A universal Arabic sign language to invent! Come." He safely secured her hand in one of his own and set off toward the front doors of the center. "Let's go find our daughter, see who she's torturing with her newfound listening skills now."

"Da'har beware!" Robyn laughed, taking a skip to catch up with her husband's long-legged strides. "Our girl is going to make the country—and her parents—very, very proud."

She relished the squeeze she received from Idris's hand at her words and, unable to wipe the smile off her face, turned to face the press who were already beginning to gather for the ceremony and gave them a happy wave.

* * * * *